TEENAGE COP

When Stephen Crosby joined the police force as a teenager, his father disowned him, but Stephen was determined to better himself. There were petty jealousies and internal pressures at the Police Station and Stephen decided the only way he could prove he was adult enough to do the job was to operate alone. When three ruffians set about robbing elderly people, young PC Crosby found himself facing sudden danger as a jagged bottle was held against his neck and he was ordered to take the villains to freedom. Suddenly, he was very much alone ...

TEENAGE COP

by

Peter N. Walker

Dales Large Print Books
Long Preston, North Yorkshire,
England.

British Library Cataloguing in Publication Data.

Walker, Peter N.
    Teenage cop.

    A catalogue record for this book is
    available from the British Library

    ISBN 1-85389-963-1 pbk

First published in Great Britain by Robert Hale Ltd., 1982

Dales Large Print is an imprint of
Library Magna Books Ltd.
Printed and bound in Great Britain by
T.J. International Ltd., Cornwall, PL28 8RW.

ONE

'Crosby.'

Stephen glanced from the desk when the sergeant called his name.

'Yes?'

'Wait outside. Atkinson ...'

Stephen moved easily between the straight lines and left the claustrophobic atmosphere of the classroom. There were chairs lined against the outer wall but he did not sit down. He didn't know why he had been sent here. The candidate called Atkinson followed and then more young men emerged, pleased to be released from all that reminded them of school.

'Why has he sent us out?' Atkinson asked anyone who cared to answer.

No one tried to reply. No one knew the answer.

Stephen waited with the others and rubbed his hands because he didn't know where to put them. Then the sergeant emerged.

'Right,' he said sternly. 'Through that door opposite, all of you. Wait in there.'

They ambled uneasily across the wide, polished corridor and one of them opened the door. It led into another room, a large and airy lounge with armchairs around the walls. There was a polished table in the centre brightened by a bunch of fresh flowers. The sergeant followed them into this cheerful place.

'Right,' he said once more. 'Sit down, all of you. All close together, not dotted around the bloody room so I've got to shake my head like one of those model dogs in the backs of cars. Here, in front of me.'

When the untidy knot of young men had settled down, the sergeant seated himself on the edge of the table with one leg swinging casually. In his hands he had a sheaf of paper which he regarded with the solemnity of a doctor.

'Fifty in there.' He pointed at the door and Stephen guessed he was referring to the examination room they'd just left. 'Ten in here. Ten passes. You lads. All of you. Good marks.'

That explained it! Stephen had wondered why they'd had to write out their life stories after the tests. Now he knew. It gave the examiners time to mark the papers, not that it would be too difficult. It was all ticks in boxes. All the answers were right or wrong, there were no half measures, no opinions.

'You lot have all passed,' the sergeant actually smiled. 'Well done. That lot in there haven't, so they've had it. They can apply to other police forces if they want, those with a lower standard than us. We demand a high standard, the best. We've the highest standards in England, so we can pick and choose. And we've the pick of the best now. Good pay, loads of kids out of work. Security. Variety, it's all there.'

He sounded like a walking advert for the force, but Stephen listened, not wanting to miss a thing. He'd passed! Him! Stephen Crosby ... a bloody copper ...

'Right,' the sergeant interrupted his thoughts again. 'This is just the first step. Next is the boss. The Chief. Chief Constable to you—sir in fact. He sees all of you next. He interviews you to see if you are suitable. He'll talk like a brother but don't be fooled. He's sharp. Brain like a razor. Sees through false stories in no time. Can't stand fools, respects truthfulness. I'll take you into his office—be smart, polite. I'll introduce you by name as you get to his desk. Stand there until he says sit. There's a chair ready. Sit down. Don't fiddle with things. If you're a fiddler, clasp your hands together. Don't pick your nose. Answer all his questions ...'

He rambled on to give the recruits the benefit of his experience as they all sat nervously in the armchairs.

'Right,' he said at length. 'Alphabetical order. Atkinson, you're first. Come with me.'

They watched intently as Atkinson followed the sergeant out of the room.

'Who's next?' asked a tall, well-spoken youth.

No one answered.

'I'm Crosby,' Stephen said eventually.

'Anyone before Crosby?' the fair haired youngster stood up and beamed. 'I'm Fairclough.'

'Welford.' 'Peterson' ...

Several names were called and each man worked out the succession of his own exit through that door to the big office upstairs.

'What do you do then, Crosby?' asked Fairclough. He spoke like a toff.

'Nothing,' said Stephen. 'I'm out of work. I left school and couldn't get a job. So I applied—and here I am.'

'University,' said Fairclough. 'Did maths at Nottingham. No bloody work for me either. I never thought I'd end up in the fuzz, not after the way we reviled them ... sign of the times, eh?'

The others joined in. One had been a salesman for a soap manufacturer, another a barman, yet another a soldier who'd left after a short-service commission. Clever men. Worldly men. Men who'd done things and been places.

Stephen looked at them. They were all tall, confident and smart, every one of them. No riff-raff. They'd all made an effort for today—clean shoes, smart haircuts, nice clothes.

He wondered if they knew he had his dad's suit on. He wondered if dad knew!

As they chattered among themselves, he thought Atkinson was a long time and began to fidget, twisting his hands as he wondered what the Chief Constable would ask. He'd never met a Chief Constable before. He'd seen them on television, talking about murders or riots in the street, but his only dealings with the real police had been at school when they'd come to give talks about drugs or when they'd showed off their dogs and horses. Sometimes he'd been chased out of pubs because of drinking under age, or chased off the streets when the lads formed big groups of noisy kids. Not trouble, just boredom, chatting harmlessly but frightening old ladies by laughing loudly or throwing empty beer cans about.

After an age, the door opened. The sergeant appeared without Atkinson.

'Crosby.'

'Good luck, mate,' one of them called as he walked towards the door, remembering not to wring his hands when talking to the Chief Constable.

'He's in a good mood today, son, so you're laughing. He'll ask about your family, your school, your ambitions. Tell him you're aiming to make the top. You'll study hard and pass exams. Lay it on thick, he loves it, but don't con him. Why did you come to join? Don't give him all that crap about a fine career ... be honest. Say jobs are hard to come by and you'd often thought about joining—tell him about seeing the dogs and horses at your school. He'll love that bit ...'

The fatherly advice continued until both men were standing outside a heavy door with a polished brass knob. He could see himself reflected upside down in the knob.

'Right—inside is his secretary. Nice woman, nice legs. His door is through her office—she keeps the riff-raff out.'

He knocked and walked in.

'Mr Crosby,' the sergeant announced.

She smiled at him, sensing his nervousness, then pressed an intercom on her desk.

'Yes?' came the soft voice from inside.

'Mr Crosby, sir.'

Mister Crosby!

'Right.'

She smiled and wished him luck. She had nice teeth and fluffy hair.

The sergeant knocked on the thick door and a voice called, 'Come.' The sergeant went in, halted and thumped his feet to attention as he said, 'Stephen Crosby, sir.'

'Fine, fine,' the soft voice answered. 'Let me see this young man.'

The sergeant beckoned and Stephen entered, doing his best to imitate the sergeant's smart marching movements. He found himself heading towards a large polished desk bearing papers and behind it sat a very smart man with immaculately groomed hair, flashing white teeth and a ready smile. He'd be about Stephen's dad's age.

'Ah, Stephen Crosby,' the Chief Constable stood up and extended a hand across the desk. Stephen shook it; it was a strong grip and the man said, 'Sit down please.'

Stephen sat on the chair right in front of the desk. He couldn't see the sergeant because he was sitting somewhere behind, well out of sight. Stephen remembered about his hands, so he clasped his sweating palms together on his lap and licked his lips as he awaited the inquisition.

'Now, Stephen Crosby, isn't it?'

'Yes, sir.' He remembered the 'sir'!

'Eighteen and a half, eh? And never had a job.'

'No, sir, there's no work about.'

'Quite. So you decided to try us, eh?'

'Yes, sir, well, not quite like that. I'd seen them at school, you see. Policemen, that is. With horses and dogs, or telling us about drugs and how to avoid cycle accidents. I thought it sounded a nice job, sir, dealing with people.'

He'd got that bit in nicely.

The Chief Constable wrote something on the file on his desk.

'You've tried to get work?'

'I'd seen the leaflets about the police, sir, saying eighteen and a half was the age to join. I tried for jobs to fill in my time—waiting on, barman, labouring, that sort of thing. But there was nothing.

I've been on supplementary allowance, sir. Dead boring it was.'

'How did you fill in your time?'

'At first, nothing. Lazing about, lying in bed till dinner time then going out to the pub to meet my mates. They were all the same, sir, dead bored. Then I got reading. My mam gets books from the library so I went down there, sir. I got reading a lot. I read the papers and watched the news, sir, on telly.'

'What sort of books did you read in the library?'

'Books about real things. The war, sir. Facts about this country and things.'

'You didn't read much at school, then?'

'No, sir. No encouragement there. They reckoned reading was sissy.'

'I see you attended a Comprehensive school and your only qualification is one C.S.E English.'

'Yes, sir. I should have worked harder. We've no books at home, you see, and it was only when I left ...'

'I understand. Now, tell me about your family.'

'I've a dad, sir. He works as a groundsman for a factory near us. It's a good job, regular hours, he's been there years. My mother works there as well, in the canteen.'

'Have you any brothers and sisters?'

'My sister Anne, she's twenty. She works in Boots on the Photographic counter, and I've a brother called Dennis. He's sixteen.'

'Will he join the police?'

Stephen laughed loudly. For no accountable reason, he threw back his head and roared. 'No, sir, not him. He's a right rebel. He's gone all punk now.'

'Has he been in trouble with the police then?'

'Not him, sir. He's not that bad, just daft.'

'And you? You've never been in trouble with the police?'

'Only getting thrown out of a pub when

I was sixteen, sir. I got a telling off and that was that. Never did it again, sir.'

The Chief Constable smiled.

'Well, if I accept you, how do you see your future?'

'I'll work hard, sir. I'd like to pass my exams and do well. Maybe join the detectives. But I want to learn to be a good policeman first—on the beat like you see in towns. Helping people.'

'The riots don't bother you then? The street violence?'

'No, sir. I think we'll put a stop to that soon.'

'Good; well, it's nice to have talked to you, Mr Crosby. Now go back outside to my secretary and she will show you to the waiting room. I'll let you know my decision before you leave today.'

'Thank you, sir,' and Stephen left the chair. He faced the Chief Constable for a moment and then turned smartly and walked from the room.

★ ★ ★ ★

'Well, sergeant?' asked the Chief Constable.

'I like him, sir. He's totally honest, a
very ordinary lad who could do well in
the right job.'

'He came second in the tests, eh? That's
remarkable.'

'They test intelligence, sir, and not the
ability to memorise facts and figures. He's
clearly a sharp lad, I think he'll do well.
He needs guidance though.'

'He had his father's suit on, sergeant.
Did you notice?'

'No, sir, I'm afraid not.'

'The cut. It was all wrong for a modern
suit. That shows he made some effort to be
presentable for today. I believe he'll turn
out to be a first class police officer. He's
got some rough edges that need smoothing
over, but we can soon do that. Yes, I'll
have Crosby.'

TWO

It was a long walk home from the bus. Stephen held his head high as he moved from the main street and down the steep hill towards the council estate. Their house was No 16 Coniston Road, a three-bedroomed semi owned by the Council and rented to his dad. Its windows had small panes set in iron frames which were draughty and rusted all the time, and the doors seldom fitted properly. There was so much hassle to get repairs and maintenance done that you rarely bothered. You had to ring up and fill forms in if you wanted a simple job like a window-pane fitted and they wouldn't let you paint the outside in your own colours, even if their colours were flaking off and causing the wood to rot. Dad rarely complained because he said the Council had given the family somewhere to live. 'It's a home,' he would say. 'We don't want to upset them.'

Stephen strode in front of the long row of identical houses, making his way along the tarmac footpath which ran between hawthorn hedges; it was parallel with the road and had little openings for each house's individual entrance. The houses had no garages—few of the occupants had cars anyway, and those who did were happy to keep them on the street. There was Mrs Flanagan with her dirty curtains and unclean windows; Ada Prescott with her immaculate house, always sparkling clean with lovely paintwork; that young couple who'd just moved in from Crennleford who were smartening the place after old Boris had lived there, even digging the garden. And his home.

Stephen looked at his own house. The brickwork was poor, he felt, it didn't look neat like privately owned houses, and if a lump of cement fell from between the bricks, the council wouldn't come to fix it. No pointing was done unless the place was falling down or letting water in, not like a private estate. There the householders did their own work, did their own painting and repairs, chose their own colours, kept dogs and cats if they wanted. He'd often wondered why Dad hadn't tried to buy a house because it seemed such a sensible thing to do. It would be theirs, their piece of property. He could be proud of his own house. He turned into the garden, noticing for the first time that it needed weeding and that the gate needed a coat of paint. As he approached the front door, he decided he would buy his own house. One day, he would be a property owner; it would be a modest place, but his very own.

The path turned away from the front door which was always kept locked and he tramped around the side of the building, a route he had taken every day from school, coming in with loads of homework to a television which never stopped. You couldn't work like that, not with all the family there, mum ironing and dad telling everybody to shut up because Coronation Street was on.

Near the back door, he found his mother putting something in the dustbin.

'Hello, our Steve,' she smiled. 'Been out?'

She would be turned forty-five, he reckoned, a hardworking woman who'd produced him, Anne and Dennis and who'd spent the rest of her life shouting at them or bullying them out of bed for school.

'Yes,' he said.

'Job hunting?' she put on the lid and turned to enter the house. He stood back to allow her to precede him.

'Yes,' he said again.

He'd said that a hundred times before. A hundred times she'd heard him say 'nothing today'. But today it was different.

'Is Dad in?' Stephen asked.

'In his chair, watching telly.'

'I'll go upstairs first,' Steve announced.

'That's his best suit!' she whispered, her eyes widening. 'Why are you wearing his suit, our Steve?'

'For the interview,' he said. 'I had to look smart.'

'What's this then? An office job of some sort? Men don't wear suits for work, our Steve.'

'I'll get changed. Is tea ready?' He began to climb the stairs, hoping dad wouldn't see him. He managed to reach the bedroom in safety and rapidly removed the suit and replaced it in the wardrobe which stood at the top of the stairs. He'd only seen Dad in it once, at cousin Cyril's wedding. Dad hated suits. He said they were for weddings and funerals and he never went out in it, not ever. The poshest place he went was the bar of the Spotted Cow and you didn't wear suits there unless you'd been to a wedding or a funeral.

In jeans and tee-shirt, he descended the stairs and felt much happier. Mum was in the kitchen pouring boiling water into the tea-pot and a pleasing meal was spread across the table. Say what you like, Mum was a good cook. 'Our Anne's going to be late, she's meeting Deirdre after work and they're going to the pictures. Our Dennis is down at the cricket field and said he'd be in.'

Stephen peeped into the living room. Dad's grizzled grey head was visible over the back of his old armchair and his face peered unblinkingly at the grey and white screen before him. He was totally absorbed.

'Has he been to work?' Stephen asked.

'Yes, why?'

'It's Monday, I thought he mebbe felt ill this morning.'

'He does feel ill lots of Mondays, our Steve, but that's not to say he doesn't do his bit. He does, he works hard for that lot down at the factory.'

'He could do better, mum, honest. Why didn't he get a trade or something?'

'He didn't want to, he didn't want to leave his mates. They all went labouring and things, it's not our place to work in posh spots, our Steve. We're not doctors and dentists or clerks or scholars. We're ordinary people, and don't you forget it. Don't get ideas above your station!'

As if he could. Dad always criticised people who got on, as he put it. Said they were scrounging off the rich, buttering up the wealthy or on the fiddle. Dad didn't like success or posh accents ...

'I'll get a chair,' Stephen said.

'Tell him it's tea-time, our Steve.'

Stephen went into the living room and said, 'Hi, Dad. Tea's ready.'

No reply.

Stephen collected a chair which stood just around the door and carried it into the kitchen where he placed it before a setting at the table. He occupied this place; the kitchen was too small to have chairs there all the time.

'Come on, Harold,' his mum shouted through. 'It's on the table.'

No reply.

'You sit down, our Steve, don't wait for him. We'll start, our Dennis will be in soon.'

She ferreted about in the top of the oven and produced a glass dish full of stew. It was liberally laced with dumplings and smelled delicious. Mum could make lovely dumplings when she felt like it. She spooned a pile onto his warm plate and added hot potatoes and green peas. Dad always had a meal at home like this, because he ate sandwiches at work. He didn't use the canteen because of the expense.

'Harold!' she shouted again. 'It's on the table.'

Finally, mum settled down and Stephen was about to tell her his news when Dad came into the kitchen. He wore his habitual carpet slippers, overalls and shirt with the sleeves turned up above the elbows.

He nodded a greeting to his eldest son and sat down.

'Salt?' he demanded.

'Sorry.' Mum left her place and located the salt cellar in the wall cupboard. Dad liberally sprinkled his meal with the seasoning and started to eat.

Steve watched them both eating in silence, a habit born of many years together in this house, in this kitchen. He must tell them. Dad would blow his top.

'Did they get that trouble with the boiler sorted out?' Steve asked Dad.

'Did they hell. A useless bloke from the firm came and didn't know what he was doing. It's still no bloody good, won't heat the water and rattles all day. They're useless, these so-called skilled men.'

'They're not going on strike then?' Steve asked.

'They will if they don't get hot water for their washing and so on,' Dad chomped at a dumpling. 'I've a job keeping 'em quiet, they want to come out. It's no good, son, not having hot water in a factory like ours.'

'The management is doing its best, surely? I mean, they brought the firm in who installed it and they've been working all over the weekend.'

'It wouldn't surprise me if the management told the firm not to get it fixed. They don't want us workers to be comfortable ... I know how those bastards think, son, they're always downing us ...'

'We had the police in today as well,' Mum tried to change the subject.

'Police?' Stephen asked with genuine interest.

'Aye,' his dad growled. 'Two bloody uniform cops and a detective.'

'What for?' Stephen wondered why the police would visit a furniture factory.

'The bosses again,' Dad growled. 'They

reckon somebody's been pinching from the stores.'

'Pinching what?' he asked.

'Paint, tools, sandpaper, that sort of stuff.'

'And have they?'

'Of course they bloody well have, son! They take it all the time—the lads borrow the stuff. Tin of paint here, box of sandpaper there, hammer, chisels ... they need it. The factory's got enough, God knows that, and the wages they pay there, it's a wonder they don't pinch more ...'

'But if everybody pinched stuff from work, you'd all be out of a job ...'

'Now don't you start siding with the bosses, my lad,' his father put down his knife and fork to shake a finger at his son. 'That's bosses' talk, that is. I've not talked to the cops, nor have the others and they won't either.'

'But why not, Dad? What if people pinched your stuff. You'd create about that ...'

'That's different, it's mine. This is firm's stuff. Our stuff, we put our lives into that firm ...'

'The firm's bosses put their lives into the firm as well, Dad, and money. They risk everything to give you a job.'

'They do not,' he retorted. 'They're in it to make money, the filthy rich. They can afford a few tools.'

'Did the police arrest anybody, Harold?' Mum asked.

'No, nobody talked. None of us will talk to a cop, luv, and you know it. Lackeys of the Upper Classes, they are. Government agents ...'

Stephen laughed aloud. 'Dad, you don't believe that rubbish!'

'Believe it? Of course I believe it! We all believe it—look at the way they pick on our pickets when we're striking, working for the bosses, strike breaking and all that.'

'They're stopping trouble, they're protecting you ...'

'Balls!' and dad lowered his head to tuck

into the remaining dumpling. 'What utter balls, son. Those bastards in blue are out to make life hell for the working man. They're paid far too much and they're always out to nick the working man, always.'

His father began a tirade against the police, pausing only occasionally to consume a mouthful of stew or a dumpling. Stephen listened in silence. He'd heard it all before and it washed over his head as he finished his meal. His mother shrugged her shoulders too; if anybody was bigoted, it was her Harold.

Eventually, Harold paused.

'Pudding?' she asked quickly.

She took a rice pudding from the oven. It was in a glass dish and had a thick skin across the top. It looked delicious as she spooned generous helpings into their sweet dishes.

'Our Steve's been for a job again,' she said in a moment of silence.

'There'll be nothing, as usual. This

bloody Conservative Government's not interested in us. It's against the working man all the time, putting folks on the dole ...'

'I got a job, Dad,' he said, looking at his mum too.

She smiled. She remembered the suit and thought it must be a good job. Maybe a salesman of some sort. She was sensible enough not to refer to the suit.

His dad looked up at him. There was clear pleasure in his grey face.

'You got one? Where? That building site down the road, mebbe?'

'No,' he said.

'It's a good job, Harold,' his mum smiled, thinking of the suit. 'A white collar job, isn't it, our Steve?'

Stephen had never considered the police force a white collar job, but mum meant something that wasn't labouring.

'No, not exactly,' he told them.

'Pay any good?' asked father.

'Well over five thousand pounds a year,' Stephen said. 'And expenses.'

'Bloody hell! I only get three, and that's with loads of overtime.' His father put his spoon into his rice pudding. 'Where is it? On an oil rig?' He chewed a mouthful of food.

'No. Dad, you're not going to like this ...'

His mother cried and stood up. 'Our Steve, you're not going abroad, are you? Not to one of the Arab places where they don't let you drink beer?'

'No, it's in England, here. At home, mum.'

'There's no job'll pay that much son. You've been conned. It's one of those fly-by-night sales jobs, I'll bet. That'll be commission, son, you'll have to work all hours, selling stuff nobody wants. That's no job, you're better on the dole.'

'It isn't that sort of job, Dad.' Stephen was enjoying this bout of bantering.

'Then what the bloody hell is it?' his

father stared at him full in the face, his mouth empty.

Stephen paused. He'd never seen his father in a temper for years, not since he was a tiny lad and got into trouble for throwing a stone through somebody's greenhouse.

'The police force, Dad. I've joined the police force.'

There was a long, long silence. His father sat opposite, staring into the face of his eldest son.

'No, son. No, you haven't. This is a joke. Tell me it's a joke ...' Dad spoke so quietly.

'It isn't, Dad. It's true. I joined today. They've accepted me.'

His father's face went a deathly white and Stephen could see him clenching his fists as his hands rested on the edge of the table. His cheeks began to quiver; he was fighting for control.

'But why? For God's sake why? Haven't I told you about them, about the bosses, about the establishment, about their colour prejudice ...'

'Yes, Dad, and I thought I should see for myself. I want to make my way in the world, I want a secure, interesting and worthwhile job and I took the plunge and applied a week or two ago. And today, I went to Police Headquarters and passed the exams, the medical too. I'm in, Dad. They'll have me.'

'Son, I never thought I'd see the day. I didn't. Phyllis, you know what I feel about the bloody police force. Did you know about this?'

'No, Harold, I didn't ...'

'Nobody knew, Dad. I didn't tell a soul.'

'Then you will never come into this house in uniform, right? I will not have me and my family made a laughing stock. A bloody copper in the family ... look, Steve, don't you tell anybody. Right? Don't you dare! Not our Dennis or our Anne. Nobody. A Crosby in the police ...

what about my mates down at the factory, fighting for their freedom on picket lines? And that lot that came today, after paint stealing? You'll be splitting on them, eh? I won't feel safe in my own house ...'

'Dad, don't be stupid! I'm not here to inform on you ...'

Dad broke his restraint. 'You dirty bloody bastard!' his father snarled. 'You bloody traitor, doing this to us ... after what we've done for you ...'

'Harold!'

But Harold Crosby rose from the table and stormed back into the living room where he threw himself into his old armchair, his head cradled in his hands.

'I'm proud of you, our Steve,' his mum said, kissing him. 'I really am. He'll get used to it in time. Leave him be. Now, help me wash up, will you?'

THREE

The police training school was marvellous. Stephen spent ten hectic weeks of positive activity. He was told how to be a policeman, how to tolerate the public in all its moods and how to fill in the countless forms and operate the computers which bedevil a police officer's life. He learned about crimes and the quaint way that English law defines them; he was shown how to tackle the interminable rows between husbands and wives, or parents and children, all such incidents loosely termed 'domestics' in police jargon. He got bruised learning about self-defence, wet learning how to save lives in deep water, and bored learning how to administer first aid.

In short, a tremendous volume of work

was crammed into that ten-week initial training course. The twenty members of his syndicate were marvellous companions and even the course tutor said it was the best initial training syndicate he'd had through his hands.

Towards the end, Stephen was posted to Pollsfield to begin his operational police career. Sergeant Fielding, his tutor, handed him a sealed envelope from Headquarters which contained his instructions for reporting for duty.

It told him to be at Pollsfield Divisional Police Headquarters at 9 am next Monday morning to report for duty. Lodgings had been found for him, and he was advised to take his personal belongings. He should travel from home in civilian clothes.

Everyone on the course received a similar letter. There was a great deal of discussion and excitement as they compared notes and from his desk Sergeant Fielding smiled at his outgoing students.

'O.K. Tonight there's a farewell do in

the mess. Enjoy it. Don't make fools of yourselves on this final night, eh? Tomorrow, you hand in your kit like the sports gear and the stationery we issued on your arrival, and at eleven you get your exam results. Lunch is in the canteen and then it's all over. Ten weeks of sheer bloody hard labour. On Monday, you all start at your new stations, and I get another thirty raw recruits. Thirty pale white faces will sit here and expect me to make them into real policemen in ten weeks. I've got to push a life-time's experience into them in ten bloody weeks, ten very short bloody weeks ...'

The farewells were sad. Big hairy men were close to tears as they stood on the tarmac near their cars, all wanting to rush home but none wanting to leave their mates. People grew close on courses like this.

'We'll have a reunion, eh?'

'Yeh—six months' time. Down at the Mucky Duck ...'

'We'll get those nurses there an' all.'

'We'll all have arrested somebody by then.'

'Or dealt with a fatal.'

'And domestics. Loads and loads of domestics. Folks like my mam and dad, always fighting and shouting ...'

And so they made their final arrangements, said their final farewells and climbed into their cars or onto the Training Centre's ugly bus. Stephen used the bus because he didn't have a car and Atkinson came with him.

They sat beside one another in silence. Each was alone with thoughts of the future and happy memories of a super ten weeks. What they'd learned had been staggering, far better than school. Crimes like u.s.i, incest, arson and manslaughter, GBH and common assault ... the Police National Computer and the computer at Swansea's Driving and Vehicle Licensing centre. They'd been told how to talk to people or calm a situation ...

'How did you do then?' asked Ted Atkinson once the bus was underway.

Stephen blushed. He did not wish to discuss his examination results with anyone. They were private; they were handed to each student on a slip of paper which itemised the practicals and the written tests with all the results. The slip contained a final percentage and a class position.

'Come on,' pressed Ted. 'I was four-teenth. Not bad, eh? I was a right duffer at school. I liked the practical stuff, dealing with accidents, first aid, that sort of thing.'

'I enjoyed it all,' said Stephen. 'It was great. The best time of my life.'

'Well come on, give! Look, if you were bottom, it doesn't matter. Somebody has to be bottom ...'

'No, it wasn't that ...'

'Top then? You weren't at the bloody top, Steve, were you? It wasn't you, for God's sake ...'

'No, I don't know who it was,' and he

paused, then added, 'I was third. 68% average.'

'Third? Bloody hell! I didn't see you swotting or mugging up.'

'I worked. I enjoyed it, Ted. It was great. It wasn't like learning at school. Somehow everybody wanted to understand things, didn't they?'

'Yeh, it makes you realise how the real cops have to work.'

'We are real cops, Ted. Today, we're real cops, you and me.'

Ted fell into a long silence.

As the bus rattled and rumbled along the rural lanes towards the railway station, Ted smiled at himself. 'A real cop. Me! Biggest tearaway in our street, I was.'

'It takes one to catch one,' laughed Stephen. 'Where did they post you then?'

'The seaside. Lovely bracing Scarford. Think of the summer, all those gorgeous birds coming there for holidays and looking for big handsome brutes like me ...'

'Rubbish. You'll be fighting mods and

rockers, or other yobs who come to smash everything up. You'll be doing battle in the streets with lefties and communists. That's what the seaside coppers do now, Ted. There's no love life there now.'

'There is, you know. Lots. I was talking to a Refresher on a course last week. He's over there. Bags of crumpet he said. Too much for one man to cope with, so I'm going to help out.'

'I'm in a tourist city, all Americans and silly people with funny hats who spend their days getting lost and asking where the best pubs are.'

'There'll be crumpet there, won't there? Foreigners. Gorgeous Swedes and Dashing Danes. Germans with their lovely legs and all those coloured chicks who wear short skirts and simply love English men ...'

'They don't love English coppers, mate. Not any more. Not after Brixton and Toxteth and all that.'

'Brixton and Toxteth was a set-up, you

heard Sergeant Little say that. A set-up by the lefties. You can't blame the cops for that, those kids were stirred up and conned into doing that damage.'

'It happened, Ted. It happened. Folks don't know the background, so they blame the poor bloody coppers for everything. Police brutality, they say. What about the brutality to us then?'

'And you'll put 'em right, eh?'

'I'll try to do my bit, Ted. I mean that.'

'You do, don't you?'

'When I look back, only a couple of years, I was like that. I hated coppers, and hated authority; I didn't care two monkeys about anything. You know what kids are like ...'

'You're a kid, you're only eighteen.'

'But I'm at work. I've left school now, I've got away from home. I'm doing something ...'

'You can't change the whole bloody world, Steve. Not anything like, mate.

44

You'll see. Out there in the big, hard world, they hate us. They do, you know. They hate us. Everybody hates us. They pretend to like us, or to understand us or to respect us, but deep down they hate our guts because we stop 'em killing each other and pinching each other's belongings.'

'My dad hates the cops. Did I tell you that?'

'Your dad?'

'Aye. He played holy hell when I joined. Holy hell. I borrowed his best suit an' all, to be smart. He didn't like that one bit. He said he'd prefer me on the dole rather than become a bloody Old Bill. That's what he said, he doesn't want me near the house in uniform.'

'Why? What's he got against coppers?'

'Dunno. He just hates 'em. He didn't give a reason.'

'He must have a reason, Steve. Maybe he's been done for something in the past. Bike without lights or boozing late maybe, or something trivial.'

'He votes Labour. They don't like the coppers, do they? Socialists?'

'Dunno. I've never got into the politics thing.'

'Me neither, but I'm interested now. There's such a bloody lot to learn about life, isn't there?'

'You're dead right, old son. A lot. And this is just the job to learn.'

'You'll keep in touch?'

'Aye, of course. And you. Give me a ring when you've settled in. We'll have a pint or two.'

'Great,' and the bus ground to a halt at the railway station. They trooped out lugging huge cases and trunks, and waited on the cold, cheerless platform. The diesel came in slowly and when it stopped they all climbed aboard. Their training-school days were over. Their real police work was about to begin.

★ ★ ★ ★

The two massive suitcases containing uniform and civilian clothes weighed heavily as he walked the final yards to the police station. It stood behind a tall brick wall, and there were two gates, one for entry and the other for exit. He used the first, walking firmly along the footpath towards the square building which squatted before him. It was positioned well back from the road, and police cars were parked in front of it. A motor cycle was propped on its stand and a large notice board said, 'Divisional Police Headquarters, Pollsfield' and beside was a smaller notice which announced 'Enquiries'. It bore a painted finger pointing to two large plate glass doors.

The path sloped gently down towards the main entrance, and he noticed the huge square windows were dark coloured to prevent anyone from seeing inside. Furthermore, white net curtains graced all the windows from roof to floor, and he knew these were for security, to contain the shattering of glass during terrorist bomb attacks. They hadn't mentioned that in the recruiting leaflets, but they'd told them at Training School because all the training school windows were like that.

He pushed open the door and found himself in a very modern foyer. On the left a counter ran the full length of the foyer, and two policemen stood behind a glass partition, like a post office. Each was talking on a telephone, and two people were seated on chairs, waiting for their attention. He wondered whether to push through, after all, he was one of them now ...

'Er ...,' he began, speaking to one who'd stopped talking momentarily.

'Sit down, sir, take your turn,' and he meekly obeyed. As he moved towards a chair, a woman came in and the policeman waved at her. 'Take a chair, luv,' he called, 'Won't be a tick.'

When he finished the call, he replaced

the telephone but it rang immediately and he picked it up.

Stephen waited. Five times, the policemen concluded their calls and each time, the phones rang again. Finally, there was a lull and one of the waiting customers approached the counter.

'Yes, sir?' the policeman addressed him, showing no signs of harassment.

'I've come to produce my driving licence and insurance,' and he pulled out his wallet. Without a word, the policeman took them from him and began to write the details in a book of some sort. The second officer concluded his call and a waiting man made his way to the counter.

'I've come to see the Firearms Department,' he said. 'It's about a shotgun certificate.'

'Wait there, sir, I'll bring somebody down for you.'

The man returned to his seat for another long wait, as the policeman began dialling the required department.

'Now, sir,' he looked at Stephen and his suitcases as the ringing tone continued in the handset.

'Oh,' and Stephen approached the counter. 'I'm Stephen Crosby ...' then someone answered the telephone.

'Sheila? Front office here. There's a chap wants to see you about a shotgun certificate. Can somebody come down for him?'

And he put down the telephone, saying to the waiting man, 'Coming for you now, sir.'

He returned his attention to Stephen.

'Sorry. What did you say, sir?'

'I'm Stephen Crosby,' announced Stephen smiling hopefully.

'And?' the policeman waited, without a hint of recognition on his face.

'I was told to come today, at nine o'clock.'

'Here?'

'Yes, here.'

The telephone rang and the constable

snatched at it. 'Front desk.'

He listened and said, 'No, I've not seen him. Try Admin. If he's not there, give Collators a ring,' and replaced the telephone.

'Now, Mr ...?'

'Crosby.'

'Crosby. Why were you told to come here this morning? Is it a condition of bail or something? Lost property? Enlighten me please.'

'No, I'm posted here. From Training School.'

'Oh!' and he laughed. 'The cases! Should have guessed. Who have you come to see?'

'I don't know. They just told me to report here at nine.'

'Who told you?'

'The Training School. There was a letter, from Headquarters.'

'It'll be Admin,' he said to himself, picking up the telephone. 'They'll see to you,' and the ringing tone was clear.

'Admin, Mr Bromley,' a voice answered.

'Front Office, Mr Bromley. I've a lad here from Training School, just arrived. Name of Crosby. Not Bing, not even looking like him.'

And he laughed.

Stephen didn't laugh. It was a very, very old joke and he couldn't even remember Bing Crosby. Not very well, anyway. A crooner or something, everybody said, a singer who sang 'White Christmas'.

'The Chief Inspector sees them. He's out.'

'Where is he then?'

'In with the Chief Super.'

'Well, can somebody come down for this lad? He doesn't know his way around.'

'I'm very busy ...'

'So are we, Mr Bromley, so are we.'

'Oh, all right. I suppose I'll have to do it. I'm in the middle of checking last month's petrol figures ...'

'Bloody civilians!' and the constable slammed down the phone. 'They can't rush, can't cope with big jobs like new recruits arriving. Hang on there, son, he's coming for you.'

Stephen went back to his seat and the policeman's telephone rang just as the woman reached the counter. She was starting to tell him about a lost budgerigar, but he had to interrupt her to deal with his new call.

'Right, I'll send someone.'

He rushed across the office and lifted another telephone, rapidly dialling a number.

'Sarge? Traffic accident in Priory Street, a woman injured by a delivery van. The call's come to me, God knows how. It should have gone to Control.'

The sergeant must have said he would send a car, and at that moment the door opened at the rear of the foyer. A gaunt, middle-aged individual came out, looked around the assembled customers and asked, 'P.C Crosby?'

'Here,' said Stephen, picking up his suitcases.

FOUR

'Nobody told us you were coming,' Mr Bromley began to pant as he climbed the stairs ahead of Stephen. 'They never do. Training Schools are all alike, posting lads to stations and never telling anybody.'

'They sent a letter,' Stephen hoped he wasn't going to be blamed for this lapse.

'It'll have got lost somewhere,' grumbled Bromley. 'You'll be wanting digs as well, I suppose? Not married are you? Not living here in town?'

'They said lodgings would be provided.'

'It's easy for them. They just say we'll do it. Right muggins we are, always having to do things last minute. What did you say your name was?'

In his loose-fitting and cheap grey suit, Mr Bromley, a civilian employee of the police, continued to climb, panting heavily en route and sometimes halting on the landings as they ascended to the top floor. After four floors, Stephen was also panting but he carried his suitcases.

'Crosby. Stephen Crosby.'

'P.C Crosby. What's your number?'

'1215,' replied Stephen.

'Twelve fifteen ... ah ... yes. They did say a new member was joining "B" Section. Admin suite. This is where all the real work's done, son. Where real problems are solved. Where they pay peanuts. N.A.L.G.O doesn't look after us one bit. Slaves we are ...'

Panting between gasps of conversation, he opened a door and entered a large, airy office with plate windows, silently indicating a chair just inside the door.

'Sit down. I'll have to sort this out. On a Monday as well, as if we didn't have enough on.'

Feeling distinctly dismayed, Stephen sat on the chair and placed his heavy cases on the floor. The office seemed too full of desks, and all were laden with paper and filing trays. The walls were heavily adorned with notices and in the corner was a small battered table bearing a kettle and some teacups.

'I'm Stan Bromley,' the man said as he ferreted among a pile of papers on his desk. 'Civilian clerk. They call me an Administration Officer but I'm just a dogsbody. Chief Inspector Goddard is in charge. He'll see you in a tick, if I can find him.'

And with that, Bromley continued to rustle the huge pile of paper on his desk as he settled himself on his chair. The telephone rang several times and each time, he gave short, curt answers, usually of a noncommittal type and said he'd ring back. He seemed very, very busy, but was doing absolutely nothing. He was giving a brilliant display of nonproductive activity.

Stephen looked at his watch. The time had crept forward and it was now half-past nine and at that point, the door opened and a big, red-faced policeman entered. He was dressed in uniform trousers with a white shirt but no jacket, and his shoulders bore three silver pips on a dark blue epaulette. Stephen leapt to his feet as he recognised him as a chief inspector, a man in his late forties.

'Sit down, son,' smiled the big man. 'You're not at Training School now. Forget all you learned at that place.' So far, he hadn't even looked at Stephen. 'Who are you? A new arrival for Pollsfield? Brand new and full of knowledge, keen and anxious to get out there and help the great British public. Is that it?'

'Yes, sir,' the man still hadn't looked at him.

'Sit down, then. I won't be long. The Chief Super wants a file on a complaint we received. Now where the hell have I put it? Stan, have you seen it?'

'The Earnshaw file you mean?'

'Aye, that's it.'

'Down in C.I.D. They came for it yesterday—something about young Earnshaw being involved in stolen property.'

'Get it will you? Urgent. The boss wants it.'

Mr Bromley picked up his telephone but the line was engaged and that meant he had to walk right down to the ground floor. They put C.I.D on the ground floor so that prisoners had less chance of escape after getting arrested and being brought here. They didn't have to be supervised on stairs, in lifts or near fire escapes.

'Now, young man,' at last the big man looked directly at Stephen who was seated nervously on the edge of his chair. 'Who are you?'

'Crosby, sir,' and Stephen tried to stand up. At Training School, you always stood up to talk to chief inspectors, because they were next to God in the police hierarchy. Those ranking higher than chief inspectors *were* gods.

'Sit down, son, bloody hell! This is

England. Number?'

'1215, sir.'

'Ah, twelve fifteen. Twelve fifteen Crosby. I'm Goddard,' and he began to sort through the pile of documents on his desk. 'Now, it'll be on young Cyril's desk. Gone on leave he has, young Cyril. Lake District, I think and I'll bet it's on his desk.'

The burly man ambled across to a deserted desk and began to rifle through its filing trays, making them desperately untidy. Finally he said, 'Got it! It was there for him to action and the young bugger's gone off without doing anything. Digs! You'll be expecting to find digs all ready booked for you?'

'The Training School said they would be provided, sir.'

'Bugger the Training School. They know nothing about running police forces. Right, two things, son. First, digs. Second, you'll have to be interviewed by the Chief Super and he's got a morning conference at half past, with his heads of departments. Morning prayers we call it. It takes about forty-five minutes.'

'Yes, sir,' said Stephen, still thinking he should be on his feet when talking to this man.

'So I suggest you lose yourself until half past ten. Have a walk round the town. There's a canteen on this floor—coffee'll be on at ten if you want to sample that. While you're away, I'll get some digs for you and I'll find out when they want you to report for duty. You're on "B" Section.'

'Sir,' and Stephen rose from the chair.

'Turn right, straight ahead for the canteen. Downstairs for the front door. See you at half-ten.'

And Stephen went out, leaving his suitcases on the floor of the Admin office.

There was an hour to while away, and half an hour before the coffee was ready. He chose the town and moved easily down the long flight of stairs. Ahead of him on the ground floor was the Front Office and he pushed open the door. The two constables were still behind their glass partition, still answering telephones and coping with a small queue of people. Everyone seemed so busy, too busy to bother with anything out of their routine. The two constables didn't even glance up as he moved past them and out of the front door.

Two police cars were cruising about the grounds and a dog handler was talking to a large Alsatian which sat looking up at him as it thumped its tail on the grass. Out here, it didn't seem so busy, these officers seemed relaxed.

He enjoyed the calming effect of his walk around the town centre. Dressed in civilian clothes, he was pleasurably anonymous and he wondered what it would be like to patrol these streets in a police uniform. The public, these ordinary people passing him by, would react differently, some would hate him, some would be nervous of his presence, others would grease around him, some would attempt to tease him and others would do their utmost to injure him. Some might even respect him.

He walked for half an hour and slid into a busy snack bar for a coffee, which was better than sitting alone among strangers in the police canteen. He returned to the Divisional Headquarters at twenty-five past ten and this time didn't join the eternal queue in the front office. He tapped on the glass partition said, 'P.C Crosby,' whereupon they pressed a button to release the security lock on the internal door. He trotted up the stairs and found himself once again outside the Chief Inspector's office.

He knocked.

'Come,' bellowed the loud voice, and he entered to find Chief Inspector Goddard on the telephone. Bromley was nowhere to be seen. He pointed to the chair and Stephen sat down once more.

From the one-sided conversation on the telephone, it was evident that Goddard was negotiating lodgings for young Crosby, and the smile on his round, happy face told Stephen it was a successful negotiation.

After a few minutes, he put down the handset and beamed all over.

'Mrs Binns, 17, Ashford Terrace. Five minutes down the road from here. Nice place, son. She's got two of our lads there already, on the same Section as you. "B" Section, that is. That means you all go out and come in together, and that saves her getting confused with our shifts.'

'Is she expecting me today, sir?'

'For dinner, or do you call it lunch? When you've finished seeing the boss, she'll be ready for you. Twenty quid a week, all meals. You get a rent allowance you know. A few quid a week, but it helps with the digs. Is that all right?'

'Yes, sir.' Twenty quid a week! He thought of Anne who paid mum a fiver for her keep, with free baths and no restrictions on hours, save a little nagging.

'Good, now that's settled, there's some work here before we see the boss. "B" Section. You've been told you're on "B" Section?'

'Yes, sir,' he had no idea what that meant.

'They're on early turn today and tomorrow. They have two days off, Wednesday and Thursday. Then it's nights on Friday. Ten o'clock start for nights. You come here and report at One Box for quarter to ten, in full uniform. Your Section Inspector is Inspector Sands, a good fellow. You'll learn a lot from him ...'

'Er, sir. One Box? What's One Box?'

'Ha! They all ask that. It's our Parade Room. Downstairs, ground floor, on the right as you come through the main door. There'll be a locker there for you. Have a look today before you leave. We call it One Box after the days of police boxes. One Box was the parent police station, you see, and outside, all the boxes had numbers. There was Two Box, Three Box and so forth. We had twenty police boxes in this town; there's not one left. You young lads rely on your radio sets now, not common sense and telephones.'

'Oh, I see.'

'So One Box tomorrow morning, quarter to six. There's no need to do any duty today—take today to settle in.'

'Thank you, sir.'

'If you like, today, you can meet some of your colleagues. They're on duty now, and when you've seen the boss, I'll call a Panda car in and he'll take you to your digs. You can have a stooge round town with him till dinner time if you like.'

'Thank you, sir.'

'Now, the boss said quarter to eleven. He's dictating letters just now. Let me see. Ah, expenses. What did it cost to get here from home?'

'One pound seventy, sir.'

'Right, we'll give you that,' and he

pressed an intercom button on his desk. 'Sandra, knock out a contingent form, will you? It's for Twelve Fifteen Crosby. He's here now. Fetch some money through—it's for travelling from his home to the station this morning to report for duty. One pound seventy.'

Chief Inspector Goddard beamed at him. 'Well, son, have you any problems?'

'I don't think so, sir. It was my digs, you see, and when to come on duty ...'

'Good. That's been sorted out. This is a good station, son. The best for young lads like you, just out of Training School. It's the busiest in the county, and we've a modern station as you can see, with all the latest gear. And a marvellous set of blokes. There'll be more work for you than you ever imagined—good, hard work. Right, are you ready for the boss?'

'Yes, sir.'

'Chief Superintendent Sinclair Lloyd. Fussy old character, but O.K. Ready?'

'Yes, sir.'

He followed the big man along the corridor to a large office marked 'Chief Superintendent' and waited as Goddard entered to pave the way. Then he re-appeared, beckoned him in, and whispered, 'Stand before his desk.'

Stephen obeyed. He walked briskly in, stood before the desk and looked earnestly at the man sitting there. Chief Superintendent Lloyd rose, shook hands and bade Stephen sit on the chair which was positioned slightly to one side of the centre of the desk. Lloyd was a surprisingly small man, with a round pleasant face and a balding head which showed wisps of dark hair. They were pulled across it like the lines of a ball-point pen, and didn't conceal his baldness. He beamed at the young constable as Goddard sat on a chair to the rear of the room.

'P.C Stephen Crosby, aged eighteen and a half. Single man. I see you did well at Training School, P.C Crosby. You have come to us with a very commendable report. Third place, beating some university graduates, eh? That is excellent, young man. Well, welcome to Pollsfield. This is a very busy station and a very happy one. I'm told you are to join "B" Section, which is our most active section. You'll enjoy the work, and I know you will get on fine with the other officers. Listen to them, take their advice. Work hard and enjoy yourself.

'There is a lot to learn, as I'm sure you appreciate. I know you have been told to forget all you learned at Training School, but I'm not sure I go along completely with that argument. Certainly the stuff you'll get involved with here is a world away from Training School theory. Learn from your colleagues, watch them. Do you drive, by the way?'

'No, sir, I've never had the money to learn. Dad hasn't got a car, either.'

'Then I'm sure we can fix a course for you. Now, as you know, for the first six months, until you are nineteen, you will work with an experienced officer. You will be on Panda patrol, and I have selected P.C Templeton as your Tutor Constable. You will meet him when you report for duty. He's a good man, so learn from him. I will be keeping an eye on your progress, and I am always available for a chat if you feel you want to talk to me. If you have any problems, personal or connected with your work, you must not be frightened to come and talk them over with me. Mr Goddard tells me he's obtained digs for you with other members of "B" Section, and I know that will help you settle in. Now, is there anything you want to ask me?'

Stephen thought for a while, then shook his head.

'No, sir. Thank you.'

'Well, it's nice meeting you. I hope your stay with us will be happy.'

'Thank you, sir. I'm sure it will.'

Stephen left the big office feeling happier than when he arrived, and returned alone to the Admin office. Bromley was there, on the telephone. Chief Inspector Goddard remained with the Chief Superintendent for a moment or two, then followed Stephen back to his office.

'There, that was all right, eh? He's a fine chap, is Mr Lloyd. Now, P.C Crosby. Your money should be ready and when you've signed for it, you can go.'

Back in the office, the necessary sum was on Goddard's desk with a form for Stephen's signature, and he signed for the cash.

'Stan,' Goddard addressed Mr Bromley who had concluded his call. 'Ring Control and get a panda fixed up to take this lad to his digs. Got the name, son? Mrs Binns, 17, Ashford Terrace. Good. Well, if you need help, come to me. Us Chief Inspectors aren't a bit like your Chief Instructors at Training Schools. We're human beings.'

Stephen laughed politely, and then Mr Bromley said, 'Panda Six is coming in, sir. He'll be five minutes.'

'Right. There you are. Go down to the Front Office and Panda Six will collect you. See you around—have fun.'

'Yes, sir, and thank you.'

FIVE

Stephen waited in the Front Office and put his suitcases on the floor as he watched through the dull plate glass windows with their array of splinter-proof curtains. The queue of new customers still awaited, albeit with a choice of different faces and problems. Very soon, a small mini car bearing the words POLICE across the doors appeared from the street and pulled up outside. A young constable in uniform but without a cap marched quickly to the front door and entered.

'Stephen Crosby?' he turned his attention immediately to his passenger.

'Yes.'

'Barr. Kevin Barr. They all call me Kev,' and he extended his hand for Stephen to shake.

'Hello,' said Stephen. 'Good to meet you. I'm Steve.'

'You're a newcomer, eh?' Barr picked up one of the cases and led the way to his car.

'Yes, just out of Training School.'

'Aye, well, forget everything they told you for a start. Out here, it's all work. You'll love it, Steve. You're in digs with me, then? Old Mother Binns' place?'

'Yes, anyone else there?'

'Me, Bruce Connaught. Brew Ten we call him, and Martin Greaves, the Carpet Cleaner.'

They had reached the car and Kevin shouted, 'The door's open. Shift those files onto the back seat.'

Kevin opened the door and Stephen saw the front seat bore a helmet on a pile of papers and circulars. It was odd, climbing voluntarily into a police car. He felt weird, as if everyone outside would stare at him because he was under arrest or being taken in for interrogation. But Kevin made it all seem so normal. They placed the suitcases on the rear seat, crushing the files, then Kevin climbed in, settled down, and fitted his seat belt.

'Always belt up,' he said, fastening the well-worn belt. 'That's a Force Order.'

Stephen nodded and obeyed. The belt required a slight adjustment, but he soon slid home the lugs to tighten it around him.

'The last person to wear that was Liz Bennett. Forty if she's an inch. Two lovely knockers. She's out today somewhere, giving another seat belt a thrill.'

'A policewoman?'

'One of two, Steve. There's her and Barbara Pearson. Barbara's been in the job since Adam was a lad. Bloody good at it she is, an' all, but she's man-daft. You'll have to watch her—she'll have you in bed before you know it. Dead randy, she is.'

'They're not in our digs, are they?'

'No, just me and Brew Ten and the Carpet Cleaner.'

Steve laughed. It was just like school, having nicknames.

'Why are they called that?' he asked.

'Brew Ten. His number is two-hundred and ten. Two-Ten for short. It sounds like that beer advert they used to have on television. Brew Ten. Two Ten. They call you by numbers here, by the way. On the duty sheets, you'll be identified by number. What's yours?'

'One two one five.'

'Twelve-fifteen. That's nice. We've got a ten fifteen and everybody calls him quarter past, or sometimes coffee break. I don't think they'll give you the same name. With your name, they'll probably call you Bing. Or High Noon.'

Stephen laughed. This sounded fun and he relaxed. By now, the car was turning out of the large double gates of the police station and it was purring beautifully through the heavy city traffic.

'Papa six papa. Ten one.' Kevin booked on the air using the coded systems. Stephen wondered if he would ever learn it.

'Is it far?'

'Five minutes' walk, that's all. Handy for the nick.'

'What about Carpet Cleaner then? His number? What is it?'

'A thousand and one. Remember that advert? It was for a carpet cleaner called Thousand and One, and it cleaned a big, big carpet for less than half-a-crown. That was years ago but they still remember the number.'

'Are they good mates to have in the same digs?'

'Yeh, great. Brew Ten's maybe a bit off at times, he's older than us. He's twenty-six or twenty-seven. Getting on a bit. The rest of us are lads—I'm the oldest of us and I'm only twenty-three. Carpet Cleaner's twenty-one, just. He had a party a couple of months back. Great.'

'And Mrs Binns?'

'Not bad, as landladies go. She's turned sixty. Little odd thing with white hair dyed blonde and a layabout son. He doesn't bother us—he's not a trouble-maker because he never does anything that'll get him into bother. Albert they call him. A Binns. We call him Dusty.'

'It's a long five minutes,' said Stephen as the car turned many corners.

'One-way streets,' replied Kevin. 'You've got to think of things like that when you're driving one of these. They don't even like you belting wrong way down one-way streets at night when there's an emergency.'

'You're on early turn today, that Chief Inspector said.'

'That's it. "B" Section is working earlier today. B means Best. Our Inspector will tell you that. Jim Sands. He's getting on for retirement now, with well over his twenty-five in. He's one of the old school, but O.K. You can trust him.'

'And is there a sergeant on our Section?'

'There's three of 'em. John Timms, Bill Henderson and Stan Wilde. Wildey is frightened of the dark, but he tried to hide it. Watch Henderson—he's not much older than me, but right ambitious. He'd book his own granny, and he's always picking on us young 'uns. He thinks he knows it all. Timms hasn't been with us long, he's just promoted and we haven't sussed him out yet. Ah, here we are, young Steve. Ashford Terrace, land of hope and glory. Old Mother Binns lives at No 17.'

They drove slowly along the street of terraced houses, most of which had tiny gardens before them. They boasted good solid wooden doors flanked by bay windows with lace curtains, and were typical Victorian houses in a typical city street. Lots of old cars were parked either side of the road and alleys ran between the houses at regular intervals.

'That one on the right with the blue door. That's Dustbin Land,' Kevin smiled, and he pulled up outside. 'Papa Six Papa. Ten five Ashford Terrace.'

Ten five must be the code for booking

off the air. They'd explained something of this code at school but he couldn't remember the details.

'Right, in we go.'

Lifting one of the cases from its resting place, Kevin led the way as Stephen followed with the second load. They mounted a short flight of steps and Kevin walked straight in without knocking.

'Ma Binns,' he shouted as they entered a long hall. 'Ma, you there?'

'In the kitchen,' came the loud response.

'The new lad's here,' shouted Kevin, placing the case on the floor. 'Stick it there, Steve, and come and meet your new mum.'

He led Stephen along the long passage which had a staircase at the end, and turned through a door on the far left. This was the kitchen, a spacious room with a large table in the centre. At the far side was a short woman with dyed blonde hair and a kindly face full of wrinkles. She was baking a pie and her hands were covered with flour, but she cheerily wiped them on a cloth and came to greet her new lodger.

'They didn't tell me until this morning,' she said. 'They're often like that. I play war with them, but it doesn't do any good. I'm Hilda Binns, but they all call me Ma.'

Kevin put his arm around her shoulders and had to stoop slightly to accommodate her diminutive size. 'She's lovely, one of the best, Steve. Ma, this is Stephen Crosby. No relation to Bing and he can't even sing. I'm a poet and don't know it! How's that? Steve, Ma Binns, your second mum. Best pie maker this side of Manchester.'

She beamed at his good humoured remarks and Stephen held out his hand. She shook it gently with a woman's touch.

'I've put him in No 3, Kevin. Can you show him up while I get this pie in the oven? Then I'll put the kettle on.'

'Anything for you, Ma,' and he hugged her briefly.

'Come on, Steve. Up to your room.'

Helping with the cases, Kevin escorted Stephen up the long flight of well carpeted stairs, and into a small room at the rear of the house. It overlooked the back of the terrace and was above a small yard containing dustbins. A rear gate led into a long alley which linked all the backs of these cosy houses, and beyond were the back doors of another street. It was not a rural view, and in no way like the one he'd left at home. He felt closed in, but would grow used to it.

'It's a nice room,' said Kevin. 'Quiet, not on the front street, so you won't be disturbed when you come off nights, except by the bloody dustbin men. They bang and clatter on Fridays, about half past eight just as you're nodding off. Anyway, this is it. Your home from home. Your castle, your kingdom.'

It was as clean and as neat as a new pin.

Although the furnishings were old and the carpet slightly threadbare, it was clean and smelled of moth-balls and furniture polish. The dressing table was a chest of drawers with a mirror on top, and there was a tall, mahogany wardrobe, whose woodwork was chipped. It also smelled of moth-balls and the door creaked when it opened. He was pleased to see there was a washbasin in one corner, for that would save time on a morning.

'Do you want to unpack now?' asked Kevin. 'I'll leave you for ten minutes, eh? Get your stuff unpacked—the bog's along the landing, right behind your room. It's not noisy, and the bathroom's next door. We're all on this floor. Ma Binns and her son and heir sleep next one up.'

'Do we have a room downstairs?'

'No, we share with them. It's a bind sometimes, especially when she wants to watch Coronation Street or Crossroads, but we manage. Dusty Binns doesn't bother about what he watches. He does as Ma tells him. You'll meet him later—he'll be down town now, standing outside a betting shop or sitting in a launderette, watching her washing perform its weekly ritual.'

Kevin went downstairs with a cheery smile, leaving him to unpack his belongings. There seemed to be a mountain of uniform which occupied lots of space in his wardrobe. Big black boots, helmets, heavy top coats, three pairs of thick trousers, three tunics, six shirts, four of them still in their packets ...

It didn't take him long to place them and he put his toiletries on the washbasin, remembering to swill his face and hands before locating the toilet and bathroom. They were very handy for his room but he hoped their noises wouldn't wake him. Then he went downstairs to the kitchen.

'Ah,' she smiled. 'Would you like tea or coffee?'

'Er, coffee,' he thanked her and sat on a chair next to Kevin. The pie had vanished and the smell of fresh baking filled the kitchen. Quickly, she produced a mug of coffee, hot and steaming. He was ready for it and sipped gratefully.

Then she sat opposite to study him.

'I've always had policemen,' she told him. 'Such good payers and no trouble. No drunkenness, no women in at nights, that sort of thing. The shifts were a bit of a nuisance at first, but I've got used to them. I don't mind shifts, Steve. You're on the same as the others, that's nice. Now it's twenty pounds a week, Saturday to Saturday. Cash please. No cheques. Most of them take their washing home on their rest days, but I'll do it for an extra three pounds. Wash, dry and iron. That's not bad. If it's just the odd shirt, or pair of socks, well, I'm not fussy about charging, but for a full week's mucky stuff, well, I've got to think of my time.'

'I'll take most of mine home,' Steve was thinking of that three pounds. 'My mum says she'll do it.'

'Good. Well, if you weren't policemen,

I'd say be in by midnight, but that doesn't apply because of shifts and having to work late. I give them all a key for the front door. Yale, it is. They let themselves in, making no noise. Get their own suppers if they want, I don't care so long as they wash up. I hate dirty pots I haven't dirtied, Steve.'

She prattled on almost non-stop and within half-an-hour had extracted all the necessary information about Stephen's mother, father, brother and sister and the fact that he had no current girl-friend. She learned all about his schooling and personal life, and retaliated by telling him all about her three lodging bobbies and her idle Albert. She wished he'd joined the police or done something useful, but he never would. She had no idea what he'd do when she died, he was totally useless, one of the nation's unemployables.

'I'm getting on, Steve, you see. I'll be sixty-two next. It's no age to be worrying about a son who can't even boil himself an egg.'

'You've been too good to him, Ma,' said Kevin and then quickly turned to Stephen. 'Now, Steve. It's gone eleven. What time's dinner, Ma?'

'Two o'clock, when you come off shift.'

'Can you wait until two, Steve?'

'Sure,' he readily agreed.

'Right, then I'll show you the town. We'll be back at two, Ma.'

The next three hours were a whirlwind of introductions, sight-seeing and advice. Stephen was told about the radio in the panda cars, the Control Room, the problems of arresting women and drunks, the layabouts in the city, the druggies, the vandals, the con-men, the petty thieves and the big-time crooks who used the city as a base. He was shown good pubs, bad dives, brothels, clubs with unsavoury clients and clubs with the posh clients. There were many garages, shops and hotels which welcomed the patrolling bobbies in for coffee or tea when they were cold and tired, but Kevin warned that they expected something in return, like help with an awkward customer even though the problem may not be a police matter.

By two o'clock, Kevin had dealt with three traffic jams, one old lady who had lost a cat, two Americans who thought they were in York; and had served several summonses from his brief case on the back seat. He never once stopped work; even though he was filling Stephen's head with advice and confusion, he never once stopped being active.

By two o'clock, it was over. The little car was parked in its allocated place at the station where it was filled with petrol for the oncoming section's patrol.

'Always fill your car,' Kevin said. 'Always keep a full tank. Check oil, water, petrol and tyres. Check for damage too. Make sure it's not damaged when you hand it over. The bloke who takes over from you might bump it and say you did it, so check it carefully.'

'You mean a policeman would blame me for damage he did?'

'You bet he would, mate. They're a right set of bastards, you know. Don't trust 'em one inch, not those off other Sections. Our lads are fine. They're great. They'll get you out of a mess, all right. Not the others. So check the car before you leave it. And make an entry in your pocket book. Write something like "Checked Papa Six Papa at 2 pm today, no damage, all in order". It's there for ever, if anyone accuses you.'

Stephen watched Kevin sign off duty. He radioed Control to make the final call which booked him off and he then checked the little car for damage and other faults. There was none. He filled it with fuel, checked the water and oil and kicked the tyres.

'That's it, then. Now we go into One Box to see the Sergeant, just to sign off with him. Come in, you'll like to meet him. They might all be there, and the inspector.'

Everybody was in One Box, signing off, handing in reports, checking radio sets and doing a host of other busy jobs. They were far too busy to notice the recruit within their midst and Kevin managed to introduce Stephen to Sergeant Wilde who shook his hand and said, 'We'll see you tomorrow then,' and walked away.

'Come along, Steve, Ma Binns will be waiting with a big dinner for you.'

Stephen realised he was hungry.

SIX

Steve felt nervous as he entered One Box in full uniform. Even though Kev accompanied him, there were the telltale signs of tension in his stomach, the quivering of his throat as he fought to control any indication of blushing and the desire to turn and run. They all seemed so confident and professional, and the fact they were deep inside a new police station didn't seem to impress any of them. They milled about and filled the room with loud chatter and laughter.

For him, it was terrifying; he remembered his childhood when his mother had threatened him with the police, and once she'd dragged him towards a brick-built station with threats of pushing him inside for misbehaviour. But now, he *belonged* here. This was where he worked. These men, all dressed like him in thick blue serge with blue shirts and black boots, were his equals, his pals and his companions. His helpers and workmates. Full of anxiety, he followed Kev as he pushed through the crowd of busy men.

'It'll be hell in here in ten minutes,' Kev shouted above the chatter and general noise. 'The late turn comes off and they all rush in to dump their stuff before the pubs shut. Come along, down here. There'll be a locker for you.'

He led Steve into an ante-room which was full of tall, slim lockers all painted grey. Each had a name plate at the top of the door.

'Find an empty one and give the number to the sergeant,' said Kev. 'Mine's 87.'

As Kev unlocked his door, Steve moved around the array of tall steel sentinels, noting those with smashed locks, rusted hinges and buckled doors. It was hard to find an empty good one but he came across number 101 which was alright. He took off his civilian jacket and hung it on a peg inside, thus establishing his claim. This would house his uniform jacket and his accoutrements like truncheon, handcuffs, torch, tape-measure and other personal items while he was off duty. He began to stock it and found Kev was at his shoulder.

'Great stuff. You've found one. Got everything you want?'

Steve nodded.

'Right, come on, it's time to meet your sergeant. It's Wilde tonight, Woolley Wilde. We call him Woolley because he can't make big decisions.'

As the men continued to mill around, organising themselves and drawing personal radios from a cupboard in One Box, Kev took Steve to the table at the far end. Behind it sat a grey-haired sergeant whose thatch was thinning but whose round, red face looked a picture of happiness.

'Sarge, this is the new lad. Steve Crosby,'

announced Kevin.

'Oh, well, er, let me see. Crosby eh? Twelve fifteen. First time on nights, eh?'

'Yes, sergeant,' said Steve, standing to attention.

'No need to stand like that here, son, it's not a training school. Forget all you learned at training school. What's your first name?'

'Stephen, sergeant.' Steve relaxed a little.

'Steve, they call you Steve, do they?'

'Yes, sergeant.'

'Good. Well, sit down on one of those chairs as I give this motley lot their briefing. When I've finished, I'll see to you.'

'Yes, sergeant.'

Steve smiled at Kev who gave him the thumbs up sign, then went off to join his colleagues.

Steve sat on the plastic chair and watched. There were policemen everywhere, laughing, joking, dressing, writing. All were busy, all were doing something which seemed important, while he had nothing to do except wait.

'Eight Oh One,' shouted Sergeant Wilde.

'Sarge,' came a return call from among the assembled men.

'See me after parade. Right,' he called to the gathering. 'Settle down, you lot.'

Some of them stopped their activities and found chairs; others ignored Sergeant Wilde's request and continued to talk and joke. That would never have happened at Training School—when the sergeant shouted, you jumped. He was God at Training School.

'Come along, you lazy buggers!' shouted Wilde. 'Time to get moving.'

The room was filled with the sound of scraping chairs, shouts, moving feet and metal doors slamming shut and after a couple of minutes, they were all seated facing him.

'Right,' said Wilde. 'About time. Now listen to your beats. Four four six, Panda One. Two Ten, Panda Two. A Thousand

and One, Panda Three. Eight Oh One, see me. Four Two Six, Town centre. Eight eight one, town centre, Two four six, town centre. Six Hundred, G.P car. Six Oh One, One Beat, Two Oh Seven, Two Beat. Five seven five, Three beat. Five six eight, Six Beat. W Forty One and W Six Nine, double up in Papa One-Seven Tango till break time, checking juveniles in clubs and pubs.'

They all made entries in their notebooks.

'Tonight,' he continued, 'there's a disco in Numbers Up until two o'clock. There's a liquor licence until one o'clock so that means there'll be trouble outside. Those in that vicinity look to it. Bring 'em in, we'll find something to charge 'em with. Watch all the clubs. There's been complaints. Councillor Staniforth has been nattering to the Chief Super about bad language from women leaving the Black Bull after Ladies Night. It's Ladies Night tonight. Fetch one or two in, we'll make an example of 'em. Check car parks for stolen vehicles. There's been a rash of thefts lately from St George's Park and from Town Hill. They're mainly break-ins by using duplicate keys. They've been found abandoned over in West Yorkshire, most of 'em. Check car parks for stolen vehicles—use the P.N.C to check 'em out. That's what it's for.'

He paused for breath, then continued. 'Burglaries. There's a lot of burglars about. Good quality homes in housing estates are getting done. Televisions, record players, radios, video outfits, binoculars, cameras, all being nicked. Somebody's getting rid of it for chummy, so check all known villains. Stop 'em in the street and give 'em a going-over. Eight Four Six, there's an enquiry for you to complete for Greater Manchester—a traffic accident. A chap who works nights in the Dane Hotel has to be seen. It's in my tray. See to that. Forty One and Sixty Nine—take time checking for young girls in clubs and pubs. Check the missing persons file—two lasses from Leeds are thought to be heading this way. Thirteen and fourteen they are and they've left home for the bright lights. The silly bitches have come here ... details on the MP file.'

'Eight eight one. Pop down to the railway station after two o'clock. See Sergeant Tanner of the Railway Police. They've been having bother with vandals and he's got some gen for us. He can't see you before two.'

'What else? Oh, a bollocking from the Chief Super. He saw two lads off "C" section this afternoon with dirty boots. Both in the town centre, both patrolling right in the public eye with mucky boots. He blew his top, so watch it. No sloppy dressing, loose ties, mucky boots, long untidy hair. B stands for Best!'

At that a mighty cheer rose from the group.

'O.K. All got P.Rs?'

Steve saw one lad put up his hand and say 'no'.

'Draw one before you go. Check to make sure it works and that it's got batteries.'

'Sarge.'

'Anything else?'

A constable bearing 48 on his shoulder raised his hand and so did Three.

'You've missed us, Sarge.'

'Ah, Four Eight, and Three. Yes, special job for you. Observations. Suspected brothel in Clairmont Street. Go up to C.I.D and see Alf Wilson—he'll explain. It's an all-night job, he says, counting blokes. Don't be tempted.'

'Not by the scrubbers that use that spot, sarge,' smiled Three.

'Anything else?'

No one spoke.

'O.K. One other thing. Twelve Fifteen, come here, son.'

Steve sat and looked at the assembled men, then realised he was being addressed. He'd have to get used to his numerical name.

He left the chair and moved to the

sergeant's table, blushing slightly.

' "B" Section, this is our new lad. Twelve fifteen. Stephen Crosby, no relation to Bing. He's in digs with old Ma Binns, and he's straight from Training School. Look after him, and show him "B" Section's the best. "B" for Best,' and they all cheered.

'Right,' shouted Wilde. 'Off you go. Twelve fifteen, stay here. Eight Oh One, you as well.'

Kev came quickly to Steve's side. 'I'm meal break at two. What time's yours?'

'Er ...'

'Make it two as well, back here. You've brought your bait?'

'Yes, sergeant. Mrs Binns packed it for me.'

'Great. Right, Eight Oh One meet Twelve Fifteen.'

Eight Oh One held out a massive hand and Steve shook it, as the sergeant said, 'Stephen Crosby, Alan Templeton.'

'Steve, Alan is your Tutor Constable. We call it T.C. You'll hear jokes about

Top Cat and so forth, but Alan will guide you through your first few months with us. Listen to him. He's a first class teacher and a bloody good copper. He'll be your shadow for the next six months at least, maybe longer. Alan, look after the kid. He's only a lad, what are you, son? Eighteen?'

'Eighteen, sergeant.'

'Wet behind the ears, no experience of life and they expect you lads to sort out the problems that society dreams up for us. O.K Alan, you know what to do. See you around. Use Papa Nine Seven Charlie.'

'Thank you, sergeant,' breathed Steve, but Sergeant Wilde was already staring at a huge heap of paper on his desk.

'This way,' and Steve felt a hand on his elbow.

T.C took him to a desk in the far corner and sat him down.

'Steve is it?'

'Yes,' and Steve nearly added 'sergeant'. This man looked old enough to be a sergeant. He was very tall and slim, probably six foot two inches tall with an athletic figure and smart dark hair. His face was slightly on the gaunt side, but his complexion was fresh and his teeth and eyes were clean and sparkling. His hair was carefully trimmed and his uniform was scrupulously clean.

'I'm Alan.'

'All those numbers confused me,' admitted Steve.

'We talk in numbers here, I'm afraid. You'll soon be doing it. There's something like two hundred of us in this nick, you see, and it's easier to write numbers in all the duty sheets and logs. You get to call your mates by numbers if you're not careful—a pal of mine once invited a colleague to be best man at his wedding and called him Six. "Will you be my best man, Six?" "Delighted, One Oh Nine", replied his pal. That's how it is.'

'And the cars, they've all got numbers?' Steve said.

'All prefixed by Papa. That's the Divisional sign. This is Pollsfield town, so all our cars are P, or Papa. The numbers are in sequence—Papa Seven, Papa Nine, Papa Two Seven and so forth, and at the end there is another letter. We're Papa 97 Charlie—C for Charlie. C stands for Centre—town centre, that is. That tells Control we're patrolling the town without being involved in any specific duty. Tango cars are on traffic duty, you see. Papa Two Two Tango would be a Traffic patrol car based at Pollsfield.'

'I'll never learn all that ...'

'Balls! It'll be second nature by the end of this week.' Alan Templeton went on to explain that there were four sections based on Pollsfield, designated A, B, C and D. In addition there was a West Side Section, or Whisky Section, which was based in a small police office on the western edge of the town. Its area embraced the new housing estates and communities on that side of town. A sergeant and five men worked from West Side.

'Tonight, Sergeant Henderson is out there, with five of our lads. All "B" Section. Sergeant Timms is our third sergeant, he's manning the Control Room this week, with a staff of lads and women. They're experts in there—it wasn't so long ago when we all took turns working in Control, but it's so complex and technical now that experts are needed. There's the P.N.C with its own V.D.U's, the Message Switching, the Incident Logging Computer, closed circuit television, Resource and Availability Computer, and all sorts—you name it, we've got it computerised in there. You'll see it and you'll get your turn to operate the gadgetry. Our Inspector is Jim Sands. Smashing chap. He hates all that modern junk as he calls it. You'll like him.'

'He didn't see us off then? I thought he would have taken the parade.'

'He's too busy for that. His office is along the corridor—he'll come to meet us later tonight, when we're on patrol. He likes to clear his desk of paper before he comes out. You've met the others on the Section?'

'Just Kev and Brew Ten and Carpet Cleaner,' he laughed.

'All at Ma Binns? Nice lads. I hope they include you in their parties and outings. I reckon they will. Now, to work. I'll show you round the nick for starters, cells, control room, canteen, inspector's office and so on. We'll talk to anyone we meet, and then we'll take to the town. There's no finer way of learning than actually doing the job.'

'Will I need my helmet?'

'Yes, and draw a radio. We might need it.'

'Er, how do I draw a radio?' he asked.

'Sorry—I keep forgetting. You know nowt—you're just out of school! They'll all tell you to forget all it taught you.'

'Everybody says that.'

'It's true, mind. Dead true.'

'It makes you wonder why they send us there.'

'It keeps somebody in a job. Now, this is the PR cupboard.'

'Pee Are?'

'Personal Radio. The sergeant keeps the keys, and he locks it after we've drawn sets. Now look inside—there's shelves for the sets, and smaller sockets for the batteries. At the bottom there's a trough for dud batteries. When you come on duty, take a set out of here, take a battery and test it. Put it in the set and operate it. Like this.'

Steve watched as Alan turned the finger knob on the set to reveal a small cavity. He took two small batteries from the cupboard and slotted them inside. They would only fit if correctly assembled, and he closed the small door. The complete radio fitted neatly into the palm of the hand and when a button was pressed, an aerial emerged. By pressing a button on the top and switching it on, he could hear the voice of someone in Control Room.

'It stays on all the time during your shift,' said Alan. 'At the end, come in here, remove the batteries and replace the set on its shelf. There's a book to sign for them—you sign them out and cross them out when you return them. Breakages—report to the sergeant. Dud batteries down there.'

'It contacts this Control room, not the one at Headquarters?' Steve sought clarification.

'Yes. This links you, out there in the town, with your local Control Room. If there's something you want from HQ, you ask Control. Say a P.N.C check. Say you see a stupid bastard driving a car round town, going like a madman up and down, and round and round, and you note his car number. Radio in to our Control and ask for a P.N.C check. That's Police National Computer. You've been told about that?'

'Oh, yes. We had a man up from London telling us all about it.'

'Good. Well, give our Control the car number and they'll check it with Force Headquarters, while you wait. The modern radios, now coming on the market, link you direct to Force HQ if you want, and the new Resource and Availability System will link you direct with Force HQ if necessary. Marvellous stuff, you know.'

'There's no number on this radio?' Steve observed.

'They call you up by your own personal number. Your shoulder number. Twelve fifteen in your case.'

'And how do I answer?'

'Right, you're on duty in town. They want you to go to a crossroads to do traffic duty because the lights have failed and traffic's blocking the town centre. They'll call you by saying "Papa Control to Twelve Fifteen".'

'And I say?'

'You acknowledge by saying Ten Four. The Ten code, you know that?'

'No.'

'Bloody hell, they tell you nowt. We don't acknowledge receipt of messages by words. We use a code. It's called the Ten Code. Ten Four means message understood. Ten Five means off duty—if you say Twelve Fifteen Ten Five at Papa Control it means you're off duty at our Control Room. Ten Nine is the distress call. Ten One is On Duty ... you'll soon pick it up.'

'I hope so,' breathed Steve.

'Anyway, the first thing you do when you come on duty is book out a radio. On top of your locker there is a tray, a wire correspondence tray. Check it for mail. If there's anything for you, it'll be in there.'

'Mail for me?'

'Summonses to serve, forms to complete, reports to submit, notes from superior officers, force orders to read, letters from girl-friends—they all go in here. Check it at the start of every shift and at the end.'

'Thanks.'

'Then you sit in One Box and listen to words of wisdom from one of the sergeants. He always allocates a beat to you, or a car. Note it in your notebook, and off you go ...'

'Where do we go, Alan?'

'Round the building first, then out into the big, cruel world. It *is* a cruel world out there, especially when you are in a police uniform. Come along, we'll start you on your road to disillusionment.'

SEVEN

The following weeks were full of action. Steve found himself in a whirlwind of activity punctuated by a rapidly changing system of work. No day was the same, there were nights, lates, earlies, days off, recalls for court hearings, special duties at weekends, football matches ...

And all the time, he was under the watchful care of Alan Templeton. Alan was a patient individual, Steve discovered. He appeared to take infinite care over the nurturing of his protegé and spent hours telling Steve about police procedures, about the jargon associated with the P.N.C, about the forms to complete, the people to avoid and the people to cultivate. In no time at all, Steve had completed six weeks' service and it was during one eventful night shift that he made a move which confirmed, in his own mind, that he was a fully professional police officer.

It happened so quickly and unexpectedly. He was later to learn that all significant events in a policeman's life happened quickly and unexpectedly. You learned to cope with the unexpected, for it was such an integral part of your work.

Alan had stopped the panda car on a patch of waste land behind the Lyric and said he had someone to see. He'd be half-an-hour, he said, and asked Steve to wait. If Control called, pip the horn three times.

Steve did not ask what his TC was doing; he knew. He knew from the other lads that his TC had a woman who lived in a tiny terrace house next door to the Lyric. Those who'd been taught the copper's craft by this slim, good looking man had learned about his numerous affairs and happily accepted them as part of life's rich pageant. And so Steve waited in the darkened car. Its lights were out and its radio burbled softly in the gloom. The time was just after midnight and the town was quiet; Tuesdays were always quiet and Steve settled down to listen to the one-sided conversations which were a feature of Control Rooms everywhere.

Quite casually, he became aware of a youth hurrying across the end of the area where he was parked. The lad was slim and athletic but the darkness made it impossible to distinguish any features, nor could he ascertain his style of clothing. But it was a youth and he was in a rush. Interested, Steve watched his progress and as he reached a short block of terrace houses, the lad halted. He looked around quickly, perhaps furtively, and then walked slowly back the way he'd come. He peered down an alley and then returned to stand before one of the little houses. Steve wondered what was happening, and guessed it was a late homecomer who'd been locked out.

Then the lad bent to the ground and

reached inside one of the tiny gardens; when he regained his full height, he had something heavy in his right hand. Steve could not distinguish the object, but after looking quickly to his left and right, the youth flung the object at a window of the house. Then he ran.

Steve heard the crash of glass and the youth ran; he ran towards Steve, towards the unlit area of the waste land and Steve watched, fascinated but hidden by darkness.

Then he remembered he was a policeman. Policemen didn't sit and watch events. They acted. He must do something. All his teaching flooded back. Powers of arrest. What offence? What was his immediate action? Blow the horn for TC? Radio for assistance? No, too late. In a trice, he had opened the car door and was running after the youth who now turned in another direction. He had some twenty yards start, but Steve was fit. Those years at school, his course at the police training centre and his weeks plodding the beat had kept him fit and he ran after the vandal, shouting 'Police, stop'.

But the fleeing youth was also fit. Steve ran for what seemed an eternity before his quarry turned down a dark alley. Steve followed with his heart thumping and he realised he had no torch. But the alley was lit; a solitary street lamp stood like a sentinel and flooded the short alley with a dim glow and he was in time to see the lad go to a door of a house. But the door was locked.

As the lad fought with the door and shouted to someone to open up, Steve closed in. Arrest? Damage? Yes, the kid had committed criminal damage and that was an arrestable offence because it carried a maximum of ten years' imprisonment. Radio? Bugger it, he'd left it in the panda. He couldn't call for assistance, he couldn't make his first ten nine call.

As he closed upon his prisoner, the lad turned to face him. He was a fresh-faced kid much younger than himself and he looked terrified. He cowered against the door of the house as Steve halted before him, panting slightly.

They were alone, a policeman and a cornered villain; two young men at the peak of fitness, each terrified of the other.

'Stay right there!' Steve shouted. 'You're under arrest ...'

The other said nothing, but cowered against the sheltering wall of the house, looking anything but menacing.

Steve moved closer and said, 'Come on, get up. Any trouble and I'll knock your head in ... stand up ...'

The other obeyed.

This was easy. His first arrest.

'You threw a stone through a window,' Steve said. 'That is criminal damage. I'm arresting you for causing damage. You are not obliged to say anything but what you say may be put into writing and may be given in evidence.'

Had he said that right? During training

sessions, they went on about the short caution and the formal caution but out here nobody seemed too worried about the precise wording. Steve knew it was important, you had to be right because defence lawyers in court would ask you to repeat it, word for word ...

He reached out and took the youth's arm in the manner he'd been taught. There was no resistance. The youth stood up and Steve found he was less than average height, a small lightly built youth with a mop of fair hair and pale features. He was dressed in jeans and a light sweater, and had training shoes on his feet.

'Come on.'

'Sorry, officer, honest. If I'd known you were there ...'

Should Steve be writing this down? He couldn't. He had a firm hold on the youth's arm and daren't let go. He might run away, then he'd be in trouble for allowing a prisoner to escape. Prisoner! This pathetic little kid was *his* prisoner ...

he, Stephen Crosby, had deprived a man of his liberty ...

'Come on, no trouble.'

Holding the arm in a tight grip, Steve steered the lad towards the waiting panda car and when they arrived, the door was standing open as he'd left it and the interior light was burning.

'Get in, back seat,' ordered Steve. The youth obeyed without a whisper.

Breathing a sigh of relief, Steve followed and sat in the front passenger seat, effectively blocking any likely attempt to escape.

Now what? Should he talk to the lad or blow the horn for TC? He'd been told not to act alone, not during his period of instruction, but he couldn't have left this crime alone. He'd done the right thing, he'd acted with speed and responsibility, and had caught a villain.

And what about the householder?

'What was that all about?' he turned to ask his prisoner.

'Sorry, honest. My mum'll play holy hell now.'

'The brick? Why break the window?'

The sullen lad did not reply, but merely hung his head. It was a look of shame, not bravado.

'Come on, you'll have to tell somebody soon.' Steve's confidence was growing. 'You may as well tell me.'

Stephen remembered to take out his notebook and prepared to take down the particulars of this incident. He should be blowing for TC but he wanted to talk to this sorry looking individual. Suddenly he felt interested in the kid.

'He deserved it,' the lad suddenly shouted. 'The bastard deserved it, I ought to kill him.'

'Who deserved it?'

'Simpson. That bastard Simpson.'

'Who's he?'

'He lives there, where I put the brick through.'

'Why did you do it?'

'He put my sister in the club, that's why. She's sixteen and he's married. He said it was safe and she let him do it; now she's pregnant and he's doing nothing. Says it wasn't him, says she's been with dozens of blokes. It's lies, all of it ... she's never been with anybody and wouldn't have gone with him if she'd known he was married and that it wasn't safe ...'

Nothing was straightforward. Steve could have done the same a few weeks ago if that had happened to his sister, but now he knew it was illegal, with a maximum penalty of ten years inside. They wouldn't give the maximum for this though; the court would probably fine him.

'How old are you?' Steve asked. Suddenly and with horror, he realised this kid might be a juvenile, somebody who had not attained the age of seventeen. That meant interviews in the presence of his parents or a guardian and all sorts of other rules. God ... he hoped he hadn't made a mess of this already. Wrongful arrest? Could you arrest juveniles?

'How old are you?'

'Seventeen.'

'Right. I'll call my mate. He'll talk to you.'

Steve pipped the horn three times and waited. TC should have been here for this ... they shouldn't let young coppers make arrests like this when there were all kinds of rules and procedures ...

'Look, mister, I'm sorry. It's just that she's a smashing lass, just got her first job. You know what jobs are like round here. Nothing. And now she's in the club because of that bastard. My mam's in hospital with liver trouble ...'

'And your father?'

'Cleared off and left us years ago.'

'All right. Now this man Simpson. Who's he?'

'Charlie Simpson. He works for Roses.'

'Roses?'

'Transport people. He's a lorry driver.'

'And he's married?'

'Yes, two kids. And now my sister ...'

'Where is she? Your sister?'

'At home. She never goes out now, she's too embarrassed. She's five months on.'

'When was she sixteen?'

'A couple of weeks back. Why?'

Steve's brain was working overtime. Sixteen only two weeks ago, which meant she was fifteen when it happened. That was unlawful. U.s.i, they called it. Unlawful sexual intercourse with a girl under sixteen, that is a crime.

He pipped the horn again, three times. TC must be busy, he must be right at the vital stages of his passion.

'What's that for?' asked the lad.

'My mate, he's out there somewhere.'

'Look, I'll pay for the window,' began the lad. 'I shouldn't have done it ... I've been to the club and my mates were laughing about it ... I got bloody angry ...'

'What's your name?'

Steve decided he must write some of this down.

'Paul Fitzgerald.'

'Address?'

'5, George Street.'

'Where I got you?'

'Yeh.'

'Date of birth.'

He provided that with no effort, and said he was out of work, on supplementary benefit and seeking a job.

'Tough, that was me until I joined up. Now, I'll have to ask why you did it.'

'I told you, because Simpson put my sister in the club.'

Steve wrote it down, expounding a little more than that brief statement. Then the driver's door opened and TC's head appeared.

'Trouble, Steve?'

'I've arrested this lad,' Steve told him proudly.

'Arrested him? What the bloody hell for?'

TC settled into his seat as Steve outlined the story and then TC quizzed the lad and confirmed all the facts given to his protegé.

'What's your sister called?' asked TC.

'Tina.'

'Where is she now?'

'At home, in bed I think. She's locked the door.'

'Let's go to your house then.'

And with no more ado, TC started the car and drove the few yards to No 5, George Street. He knocked loudly at the door and a bedroom light appeared. A girl's voice called, 'Is that you, Paul?'

'He's here, this is the police,' announced TC loudly.

There was no reply, and then they heard the door being unlocked. A young, tousled haired girl confronted them, hugging a dressing gown about her thickening body.

'Paul ...' she cried.

TC pushed past her and went into the house, followed by Steve who clung like a limpet to Paul Fitzgerald. TC found his way into the sitting room and everyone followed. Tina was crying and saying, 'Look, what's happening ...'

When they were all inside, Steve released his prisoner and stood at the sitting room door, while TC took the floor near the fireplace and addressed the brother and sister, two terrified children.

'Tina, your brother has just thrown a brick through Simpson's window because of what he did to you. It was Simpson, wasn't it?'

She nodded.

'Nobody else? Have you had sex with anybody else?'

'No, it was the first time, sir ... I didn't know about being safe and things ...'

'Fair enough. Look, you were fifteen at the time?'

She nodded.

'That makes it a crime for him, and if we prosecute it means you will find it easier to get maintenance payments off him. As it is, he'll deny it. All he need say is that you'd been with other blokes, you see ...'

'But I haven't ... not one ... ever ...' and she burst into tears.

'Steve, get onto the radio and call one of the wopsies down here, will you?'

In the absence of the girl's mother, it was necessary to interview the girl in the presence of a policewoman. Stephen went outside to the car and asked Control to send either Barbara or Liz to this house. One of them would be directed here immediately.

Back inside, TC said, 'You've got Paul's particulars, Steve?'

'Yes,' agreed Steve.

'Right, we won't arrest him, Steve. It means too much hassle and paperwork and it means taking him to the nick, putting him in a cell, getting the sergeant to charge him and bailing him out to a court. As it is, we just report him for summons. It's a minor offence—smashed window, worth a few bob. O.K? So, Paul, we've got to report this damage. We'll submit a report to our bosses and you might get a summons to appear before a court, charged with criminal damage to that window. If you plead guilty I reckon you'll be fined a few quid—a fiver or so, I think. Nothing more.'

Paul nodded in understanding.

'Now you, Tina. A policewoman is coming here. That Simpson chap committed an offence when he had sex with you, because you were under sixteen. She'll tell you all about it.'

'I don't want a fuss ...' the girl began.

'A crime has been committed,' said TC, 'so I'm afraid we must deal with it according to the law. Now, when our policewoman comes, tell her all about it.'

Barbara Pearson, mature and oozing sex-appeal, arrived fifteen minutes later and smiled at TC and Steve. 'You lads go and make a cup of tea,' she said, 'while I chat to Tina.'

And so the men adjourned to the kitchen, where Paul made a good job of fixing tea for everyone, complete with biscuits from a tin. As they drank it, Steve felt sorry for these youngsters. Here were two kids up to the necks in bother. He could have been like that ...

Three quarters of an hour later, Barbara joined them, with a tearful Tina standing behind.

'I've got a full statement from Tina,' Barbara smiled and her eyes flashed at Steve. She stood very close to him and he could smell her perfume. 'I'm going to see her mother in hospital tomorrow; I've explained about the tests we can make to establish that Simpson is the father.'

'Right, well, there's nothing more from you two right now,' TC said to the pair. 'Get yourselves to bed and we'll see you again soon. And Paul, even if you are upset and angry, don't take the law into your own hands. Right?'

Paul smiled. 'It's worked though, hasn't it? You're going to get Simpson?'

'We are. Yes, it's worked, but it could cost you a quid or two!'

'I don't mind that, not now.'

And they left. Barbara said goodbye and returned to the station to report the u.s.i to the sergeant, while TC said, 'Right, Steve, now for Simpson.'

The damaged house was all in darkness, but the lights of the panda car picked out the broken downstairs window. There was a gaping hole in the pane but the brick was nowhere to be seen.

'It's a wonder they didn't wake up,' commented TC as he knocked on the door. 'You'd think window smashing would wake the neighbourhood.'

He knocked again, louder this time and still there was no reply. His next approach was to peer through the window where he saw the remains of a fire burning in the grate. Somebody was in.

'If you don't succeed at first, try, try and try again, then have a go at the back,' smiled TC. His knocking produced no results so he walked to the rear and banged again. This time he did achieve something. A light came on above the back door and a woman's head appeared. He shouted and she opened the window.

'Mrs Simpson?'

'Yes, who is it?'

'Police,' he said. 'Is your Charlie in?'

'No, he's at work. Why?' She wore no teeth.

'We want to talk to him.'

'What about?' she poked her head out and they could see the mass of curlers clinging to her head.

'Somebody's smashed your front room window,' he said. 'It's about that.'

'Smashed my window? When?'

'Tonight. We've got him.'

'I didn't hear anything, honest ... I sleep at the back ... he's at work is our Charlie. Roses Transport.'

'Thanks, I'll try them.'

And they left.

'We could try tomorrow,' said TC in an informative manner, 'but when you're interviewing villains, you get 'em by surprise. If we leave this, she'll say we've been and he'll cotton on to why the window's been broken, and that means he'll work out some sort of story to deny being with that lass. So we'll go to Roses and catch him at work.'

The night duty watchman at Roses Transport Depot listened and told them that Charlie Simpson was not at work. None of the lorries was on the roads now, except one down in the Midlands but even it was laid up for the night. Simpson had finished at ten o'clock.

'Is his car here then?'

'Van. He's got a blue van, a Ford Transit. Battered it is. He went home in that.'

'Thanks,' said TC.

'Any message?'

'No, we'll see him later. Somebody's put a brick through his house window, that's all. Not serious.'

'Some daft buggers will do anything for a laugh,' chuckled the watchman.

Back in the Panda car, Steve asked, 'What do we do now? We'll have to wait until tomorrow, won't we?'

'We still haven't got you thinking like a copper, have we? Think, Steve. This man's a villain, isn't he?'

'I wouldn't say that, Alan, just because he's put a girl in the family way.'

'I can sense it, Steve. You'll have to develop a sixth sense, a copper's nose. Look, he's put this kid up the stick. How many more has he done? Then we go to his house and his wife says he's working late. So we try the firm, and they say he's gone home. So where is he? He's lying to somebody, maybe both.'

'With another woman, maybe? Or another young girl?'

'But we don't know, do we? So we wait—at his home. We wait and find out where he's been, we catch him by surprise. He's got a van, the man said. Not a car or a motor bike, but an old nondescript van.'

Steve thought he guessed TC's line of reasoning, and was content to sit in the panda car which was once again parked on the patch of waste land behind the Lyric. At three-thirty that morning, they saw a dark blue Ford Transit van arrive at the house. It drove past, indicated left and turned into a lane which led to the rear.

'Come on,' said TC. 'Bring a torch.'

Running in the darkness, the two policemen raced to the rear of Simpson's home, making sure they moved in the shadows. They were in time to see the big blue van vanish into a garage and as they reached it, Simpson was closing the doors.

'Charlie Simpson?' asked TC, shining his torch into the florid face of a big man.

'Aye, so what? Who's that?'

'Police,' said TC. 'Let's have a look in that van.'

'Bugger off, both of you,' and he tried to slam the doors.

But TC reacted swiftly; in a trice, he had seized Simpson and propelled him into the garage where he pressed him against the side of the van.

'No trouble, Mr Simpson, just a look inside your van. Steve—shine a light inside and let's see what we've got.'

Nervous and shaking like a leaf, Stephen Crosby shone his torch through the rear windows of the big vehicle. It was full of television sets, radios and music centres.

EIGHT

Three weeks later, Steve was in Pollsfield Magistrates' Court during the hearing of the case. The events which had led from that fascinating night with its smashed window into today's court were exciting for Steve as he listened to the evidence against Charlie Simpson. He faced several charges of burglary and theft, plus one offence of u.s.i with a girl under sixteen. For Steve and Alan, it had been a good night's work.

Steve had to give evidence of being present with P.C Alan Templeton when he'd found the stolen goods. Alan gave evidence of the smashed window, the interviews with young Paul Fitzgerald and the discovery of the vanload of hot property. As the evidence was presented to Their Worships, Steve recollected the aftermath of that night. Alan had implored him not to reveal his absence at the crucial time because it could have landed him on a disciplinary charge. The narrative of events had to make it appear they had both been involved. And so the story was concocted with the final report saying that Alan Templeton saw the vandalisation of the window, gave chase, made the interviews and investigated the complaint by the sixteen-year-old girl. The climax was the swift arrest of a highly professional thief.

Finally, everyone waited for the magistrates to deliver their sentence. The fellow's guilt was never in doubt, and Alan had explained how the case could have gone to Crown Court had Simpson requested it. Simpson, however, knew the value of getting cases heard before the local bench whose members were far more sympathetic and could be conned into delivering light sentences or even periods of probation. At Crown Court, a villain risked meeting a crusty cold judge who dished out prison sentences as if they were sweets.

Eventually, the magistrates filtered back into court and the chairman sat in the central position in a high-backed chair.

He waited until everyone was in position, and called for the prisoner to stand up.

'Charles Edward Simpson,' he began. 'We have listened to all the evidence and have no hesitation in reaching our verdict. Yours has been a shocking catalogue of crime and greed, and upon the evidence presented in this court today, the bench has no hesitation in finding you guilty of all offences charged. Have you anything to say before sentence is passed?'

Simpson shook his head.

'Has the defendant any record?' asked the chairman, addressing his question to the police officer who prosecuted.

'Yes, Your Worships,' and he proceeded to read out a formidable list of convictions, chiefly comprising theft, handling stolen goods and burglary, all over a period of ten years. There were five motoring convictions, and two for indecent assault on young girls.

At the conclusion of this list, the chairman went into a huddle with members of the bench and finally addressed Simpson.

'Charles Edward Simpson, this court does not have the power to sentence you to a lengthy term of imprisonment, but it is felt that your past record and your current crime should be considered by a higher court. For that reason, you will be committed to the next Crown Court for sentence on all counts. You will remain in custody until that hearing.'

'Bastards, you callous bastards ...' Simpson shouted, but two police ushers seized his arms and escorted him protesting all the way to the cells.

Alan Templeton smiled and raised his thumb towards young Steve, but the chairman had not finished.

'Inspector,' he addressed the prosecuting police officer. 'This court feels that the work, initiative and devotion to duty shown by P.C Templeton deserves commendation. For that reason, this court wishes to commend him for his prompt action which led to the arrest and conviction of this determined criminal. I trust that my remarks will be brought to the notice of the Chief Constable. In addition we feel it is gratifying to learn that a novice police officer was with this experienced constable throughout the investigation of these offences. We trust that P.C Crosby will benefit from his association with P.C Templeton.'

There was no commendation or word of thanks for Steve. Not a mention. Not a thank you. He looked at Alan, but Alan was shaking hands with the sergeant and the inspector, and was being patted on the back by a journalist. As Steve left the court, he felt lonely and dejected, and realised he'd not even managed to record his first arrest because Paul Fitzgerald had been reported for summons. Poor Paul—he'd been put on probation for breaking that window, but it was his actions which had led to this marvellous arrest.

Back in Ma Binns' house, he was comforted by Bruce Connaught, alias Brew Ten. Bruce told him how officers seeking promotion rode on the backs of keen young officers; they signed all the charge sheets, arrest forms and offence reports in order that their names were always in the limelight. He told Steve not to allow Templeton to play that game again.

'The C.I.D are the same, mind,' he went on over a cup of tea. 'Never tell 'em owt, lad. If you get first wind of a crime, keep it to yourself and make your own enquiries. If you whisper to the jacks, they'll zoom in and make the arrest. You'll never get a sniff, not one.'

'But isn't it our job to get the C.I.D to

the scene of a crime?'

'Aye, but we all tell 'em *after* we've made the arrest. Then the arrest is chalked down to us. If it's a non-starter job, one where there's not likely to be an arrest, then fetch 'em in. Let 'em chalk all the unsolved ones against their names, lad. That's what they're paid for. The uniform lads make all the best arrests anyway—just remember the Black Panther and the Yorkshire Ripper. All the C.I.D bull-shit in the bloody world didn't catch them. We did. The uniform lads.'

'But we're all in the same job, Brew Ten, surely?'

'I know, you know, but do *they* know? They aren't interested in the crime rate—they just want to feather their own nests and get promoted by using you. Remember, tell 'em nowt, lad. Nowt.'

'It doesn't make sense, Brew Ten. I mean, if I'm in uniform and somebody tells me that a local villain has nicked something, aren't I supposed to tell C.I.D?'

'You're *supposed* to, but you don't. You nick him, then tell C.I.D.'

'But I've not been taught about crime procedures. That Simpson case lost me, what with all the jargon about T.I.C's and so on. I don't think I could arrest a thief ...'

'You just grab him, lad. Fetch him in. The sergeant in the charge room will sort something out. Don't forget the evidence—they try to get rid of evidence in our cars—they push stolen watches down the sides of the seats, push drugs under carpets, hide knives they use to rip open the guts of their enemies, or your guts. Search first, arrest and fetch in. Think of Number One—that's you. Get some arrests under your belt, lad. Public order, section five, breach of the peace, going equipped, loitering. Things like that. That's how to make your mark in this world.'

'Thanks, Brew Ten,' and he went upstairs. He lay on his bed for a long time without removing his boots and uniform trousers. He thought about the events of recent weeks. Certainly, TC's behaviour over the Simpson arrest had been selfish—he could see that now. It had been a hard lesson and it hadn't been easy trying to learn the procedures from a seasoned policeman only to find yourself left out when the praises were sung.

A few days later, Steve was off duty and enjoying two free days in the middle of the week. He found it refreshing to walk through the town in old jeans and a tee-shirt and to sample coffee in coffee houses or drink pints of ale with Carpet Cleaner, Brew Ten and 446. But today, he was alone; he'd accrued a good deal of overtime, some of it because his court appearance had fallen on a day-off, and he had been told to take today off duty to use up the time he was owed.

For once, he found it pleasant to walk alone and not in a gang of pals who moved together, stopped together, ate together and drank together. He window shopped, he moved into the department stores, the book shops, the record shops, the gents' clothes shops and many more, idling his time and enjoying the relaxation. He wondered how many people around him knew he was a copper. Not many; maybe the short, tidy hair style gave him away? The lads at the nick said short hair meant you were either a soldier, a copper or a discharged prisoner. Jeans and tee-shirts didn't look like cops' clothes, not in his view. He remembered that old copper in the town where he lived as a child; you could always tell him off duty. He always wore smart clothes and polished shoes, and he walked tall. Upright, his mum said, upright with bearing. Policemen always used to look the part, even when off duty, but not any longer.

Thinking about clothes made him turn into a shop called HIM. The wide frontage was completely open and loud music sounded from inside where low lights and bright colours welcomed prospective customers. Steve strolled in, hands in his pockets, as he sauntered among the circular stands of shirts, sweaters, jeans, jackets, underclothes and fancy hats. It was a young man's emporium, highly colourful, but cheap and attractive and he decided he should buy something. He hadn't bought himself any clothes since joining the Force—his uniform meant he was adequately clothed for work, and his older clothes, bought by his mother, satisfied his off-duty needs. But they were getting shabby, tatty and dated. He thought of that old policeman and the smart suits he always wore. He didn't want to look typecast or dreary.

Did this shop stock suits or conventional jackets and shirts to wear with ties? He moved about the noisy gloom, twirling stands of sports shirts or swimming costumes, and then he noticed two youths among the jeans. They were younger than him, probably sixteen, and they were lifting the legs to examine the width of the bottoms, taking samples off their hangers and holding them against their bodies. They were moving around, looking at other samples, taking the jeans with them. Two men with four pairs of jeans.

Then he realised their constant turning of heads was furtive behaviour, that the jeans were being pushed up their sweaters ... he remembered Brew Ten's talk about evidence ...

Where was the assistant? He was at the other end of the shop, deep inside and not close to the door like these lads. He was busy talking to another youth who was examining a denim jacket and was totally unaware of the conspiracy being played out behind his back.

Steve must act. He couldn't allow this to go on.

He moved from behind his sheltering stand of trousers from where he had a clear view but they hadn't seen him. The assistant, a middle-aged man about five

145

feet five inches tall, looked strangely out of place here and he was still engrossed with his customer. The youths now moved to the rack of socks near the entrance and as Steve watched, they stuffed pairs of brightly coloured socks up their sweaters, supporting their loads with folded arms to conceal the growing bulk.

That was enough.

Steve moved out. He began to walk quickly towards them, but they must have sensed it was time to leave. Acting in unison, the pair moved towards the open frontage where the crowded street would soon swallow them and provide a haven of safety.

'Hey!' he shouted, hoping to attract the attention of the assistant.

They ran. The two youngsters bolted from the shop and Steve gave chase; he was aware of the shop assistant also running the length of the shop, but the lads were agile and swift, having planned this venture. They wove between the startled pedestrians as Steve shouted, 'Stop ... stop them ...'

No one attempted to halt their onward rush, but one of them stumbled over a drain cover. He pitched headlong to the footpath, landing face down at the feet of two startled men. They simply stared at the prostrate figure and as he attempted to rise, Steve closed in. The other youth had vanished, and as the breathless thief fought to gain his feet, Steve was upon him. He threw himself at the still struggling lad and brought him crashing to the ground for the second time as the two astonished gentlemen continued to stare.

'On your feet, mate,' he said. 'Police, you're under arrest for stealing.'

'Stealing, balls!' panted the other, struggling in Steve's firm grip. 'I bought this lot.'

'I saw you and your mate in the shop. Come along, you're under arrest,' and he forgot all about delivering the short caution. Keeping a tighter than necessary grip on the youth's arm, Steve marched him back to the shop as the tiny, pale-faced assistant came out to meet him.

'I've called the police,' he said. 'They're sending somebody. Thank you, young man ... thank you.'

'Can we take him inside?'

'Why of course. Yes.'

Steve led the youth into the shop which was now devoid of customers, and took him to the rear of the premises, close to the partition which acted as office and rest-room.

'Stand there,' he ordered the prisoner and pushed his hands up the commodious sweater. Out came a pair of jeans, three pairs of socks and a tee-shirt.

'Did you pay for these?' Steve asked him.

No reply.

'Did he?' Steve asked the assistant.

'No, certainly not.'

Stephen placed the haul on the tiny counter and said, 'I'm P.C Crosby from the local police station. This man is under arrest for stealing from your display. do you recognise these as your property?'

The little assistant held up the items and nodded briefly.

'Yes, they are ours,' and as Steve placed the goods together on the counter, the prisoner suddenly lunged at him and struck him deep in the belly with a closed fist. The sudden blow caught him utterly by surprise, winded him and knocked him into the little man who teetered backwards and in the ensuing commotion, the prisoner darted to freedom. He galloped through the shop, pulling mobile rails of clothing behind him as he ran and in a trice, he had reached the crowded street.

Steve was winded. The blow had knocked every puff of wind out of him and he stood bowed in the shop, retching and panting for breath as the little man gave chase. But it was futile.

Steve remained on his knees, trying his best to recover his breath and the little man returned with a sorrowful expression.

'I'm so sorry, officer, he's gone.'

'Sod it!' Steve managed to mutter. 'Sod it!'

'No, look ...' the man helped Steve to his feet, 'are you all right? It was good of you ... I'm not the usual person ... my son looks after this shop and he's ill today ... I'm not used to people like that, thieves and violence.'

Steve tried to speak but the words failed. He fought for his breath, standing doubled up in the confined space as he expanded his aching chest and lungs to fill them with air. That kid had either known exactly where to strike or he'd been very lucky.

The sound of a car drawing up outside caused him to look to the street and a panda car was drawing up.

'Your colleagues are here,' smiled the man. 'I'll bring them in.'

It was Sergeant Henderson and W/P.C Pearson.

'Where is he then, Twelve Fifteen?'

'He got away, sergeant. I chased him ...' the action of speaking made him pant heavily. 'I caught him ... got him in here ... this is the stuff ... then he hit me in the belly ... winded me ... ran off ...'

'Bloody hell! You mean you let a prisoner escape?' Sergeant Henderson began to shout.

'Sorry, sergeant, it was so sudden ...'

'He couldn't help it,' the little man came to his rescue. 'It was so sudden ... I was in the way ...'

'It is a disciplinary offence to permit a prisoner to escape, Twelve Fifteen,' chanted Sergeant Henderson. 'Of all the bloody stupid things to do. You've let a good one go—caught bang to rights and you mess up the job. What a bloody thing to do ...'

'Go easy on him, sarge,' said W/P.C Pearson. 'He is off duty and he has taken a knock.'

'We could have had this one chalked up to us. An arrest red-handed. Shoplifters nicked with the stuff. And what happens, Twelve Fifteen? You let him go. You release the villain. You'll be the laughing stock of the local villains now, you realise that?'

'He hit him, sergeant, very hard ...'

'Did you get a description?' Henderson asked the little man.

'Er, no. I hardly saw them, sergeant. Just young men in jeans.'

'And you, Twelve Fifteen? Can you describe your missing prisoner?'

Steve was standing fully upright now and had to shake his head. 'Not really, sergeant. It all happened so quickly ...'

'Take him home, Forty One. You live nearby, don't you? Take him for a cup of tea. He needs it. Whisky would be too strong for him. We don't like weaklings on "B" Section, Twelve Fifteen. Let a woman look after you ... go on, out. I'll walk back. I'll have to think of something to tell the inspector.'

As Steve walked painfully from the shop,

Barbara Pearson said, 'The car's outside, Stephen.'

In the car, she soothed him and tried to cheer him up, saying that Sergeant Henderson's bark was worse than his bite. 'He's had a bad day, Stephen. He's been before the Superintendent for his annual assessment and didn't get a good one. He sees his promotion chances sliding away; he's a good copper, Stephen. Hard, but good. Ambitious and careful. He'll calm down—next time you see him, he'll have forgotten all about this. And don't you fret—we've all let prisoners go like that. All of us, on duty too.'

She prattled on as she drove the panda car through the busy streets and out towards a lovely semi-detached house in an avenue near the southern outskirts.

'My home,' she said. 'Come in.'

After locking the car and booking off duty, Barbara showed him into the kitchen and through to the comfortable lounge where she lit a gas fire.

'Tea?'

'Fine,' he agreed. A cup of hot, sweet tea was just what he fancied.

'I always think a cup of tea does wonders,' she was talking from the kitchen. 'It's a form of shock you've got, that blow to the belly. It really knocks you up, eh? All part of the job, though ...'

Five minutes later, she emerged carrying a tray with two cups of tea and some chocolate biscuits which she placed on a coffee table. She chattered endlessly about the job, the risks, the personalities and her ideas of successful policing. She'd been in the job fifteen years, she said, and was still learning. She told him never to trust a villain, not one inch, not even half an inch. If they were under arrest, you made sure they stayed under arrest.

After twenty minutes he felt better, albeit considerably dejected and very miserable. He wondered what his pals would say; he wondered what the inspector would say and he wondered if all the villains of Pollsfield were laughing at him. How could he know the thief would take off like that? And that thump was so hard and accurate ...

'Look,' Barbara was saying. 'You need cheering up. I'm off at two this afternoon. You're off all day, so why not come round tonight? I'll fix you some supper. How about that? Steak? You like steak? With all the trimmings? I've a nice bottle of Beaujolais and we can crack that, you and me. That'll cheer you up, and I'll tell you all about some of my disasters. Eight o'clock?'

'Well, I er ...' he remembered what the others had said about the man-eating reputation of this mature woman. She liked youngsters, she would teach him all he wanted to know, and he did sincerely want to learn.

'I'll guarantee you'll feel happier afterwards,' she smiled.

And he heard himself agreeing to join her.

NINE

'You're going where?' cried Kevin Barr.

'Barbara's, for supper,' Steve blushed, knowing what he was thinking. 'She asked me.'

'She asked you? Of course she asked you. You're young and fit, and she eats young and fit men. Eats them, Steve. For breakfast, dinner and supper.'

'She was good to me.'

'So she was good to you. Fine. She has bloody good reason to be good to you—she's short of a man, Steve. She doesn't want you—she wants your body. Have you ever had a mature woman? She's thirty-five, you know, she's been around. It's not love or anything like that.'

Steve was blushing furiously. He'd never

had sex with any woman and didn't think she really wanted him like that, it was just a friendly meeting, a way of making him feel better ...

'I think she's nice,' he began. 'Friendly.'

'Next thing you'll be falling madly in love with her, like others have before. She's poison, Steve, honest. Once she gets her claws into you, she never lets go, not until she gets something better.'

'I can't back out now, I've promised I'll go.'

'Say we'd fixed something else.'

'I can't, she'd smell a rat. Look, Kev, thanks. I know you mean well but I am grown up. I'm a bloody copper, mate, not a school-kid. I can handle myself.'

'I'm offering sound advice based on what I know. She'll have you in bed before you know it and once that happens, she's got you.'

'I might enjoy it ...'

'You will enjoy it, I'll guarantee that. She's great, the best, the most experienced.

She's a raving bloody nympho to be honest.'

'Then she's just what I need!' and Steve smiled at him, the smile of a man who looked forward to a new experience. If she was all Kev said she was, it would be better than a sexy magazine.

'You need her like you need a hole in the head. There's other women, Steve, other youngsters. Look at the typists in our nick, the clerks, the control room lasses. Young and beautiful, innocent as new born babes, most of them. You could find one of those, your own age. That bloody woman's old enough to be your mother. What are you? Eighteen? Nineteen? She's thirty-bloody-five.'

'I've made my mind up. I'm going.'

'O.K, but don't say Uncle Kevin didn't warn you. Best bib and tucker, eh? She'll soon have those ripped off, mind. You'd be better going in jeans and a tee-shirt, then it doesn't matter if she rips them off in her mad lust for your virile young body.'

'Give over, Kev. It's a meal with a friend, no more.'

'Like hell it is. Anyway, you enjoy it and learn. You're here to learn, aren't you? A teenage cop about to learn an important lesson about life. I'll tell you what, Steve, it'll be a lesson you'll never forget!'

They laughed about it and spent half-an-hour cleaning their boots and pressing their uniforms ready for the next tour of duty. It was surprising how the heavy serge creased and how dusty and grimy black boots became. If there was one thing Inspector Sands demanded, it was smartness on duty with clean clothes and a well-groomed appearance. It was good for morale too because it made them work, and gave them something to grumble about.

Brew Ten and Carpet Cleaner thought it hilarious that Steve had accepted Barbara's generous invitation, and asked if he needed a photographic record of his wineladen meal with the sexy woman. For two hours that evening, he suffered the taunts and ribaldry of his mates in the digs, more so when he began to wash and shave and look for a clean shirt and underpants.

With their laughs and good natured taunts ringing in his ears, he caught a bus across the city and arrived at her home feeling distinctly nervous and very tense. Their banter hadn't helped. He rang the bell and she answered in a moment; she was wearing a long black dress with a deep neckline edged with red. A red ribbon was tied in her dark hair, now pulled back in a type of bun and she exuded a whiff of strong perfume as she stepped back for him to enter. In his jeans and tee-shirt, with an old brown leather jacket on top, he felt like a tramp at a hunt ball, but she didn't seem to mind.

'Hang your coat in the hall,' she invited, 'then come through.'

He found an empty peg and allowed his battered jacket to dangle there before smoothing his hair and brushing any unseen bits of dust from his clothes. Feeling under-dressed, he followed her into the lounge where a coal fire glowed in the grate; the lighting was subdued and her room exemplified comfort and homeliness.

'Sherry?' she asked, her eyes sparkling.

He'd never had a sherry but nodded and smiled his acceptance. She produced two bottles and asked whether he wanted it sweet or dry. He had no idea, but said sweet. She poured it into a tiny glass and handed it to him. She followed suit with a glass of the other, a pale copy of his drink, and raised her glass. 'Cheers,' she smiled.

'Cheers,' he responded, sipping gently. It wasn't anything like beer.

'Here's to no more escapes from custody,' she laughed happily. 'What did Inspector Sands say?'

'Not a lot,' Steve explained. 'He said I had to be more careful next time, and that I'd learned a lesson. He gave me something of a bulling but followed with thanks for getting the blokes in the first place. He said it could happen to anyone. I thought he was quite nice about it.'

'And Bill Henderson? He seemed a bit sore.'

'I've not seen him since then. Will he get over it?'

'He will, he always does. Ignore him—he was just upset that his section had missed a good arrest. They think like football managers, those sergeants, always wanting their section to be top of the league. We can't all be top.'

'Are we top?'

' "B" Section? We're always top, Steve. Always. The best. You'll see.'

'How can they judge us? I mean, there isn't a chart, is there?'

'Nothing like that. Just a feeling. You know, we get the arrests, the crimes, the traffic accidents. We're busy. Things seem to happen when we're on. Like that job you and Alan got, then that carry-on in the shop. Things happen to "B" Section.'

'I'm glad I'm on this section.'

'So am I,' she oozed, coming closer. 'More sherry?'

He looked at the glass. It was half-empty and he nodded. It was quite potent, he found, and very pleasant. She poured a second generous helping in both glasses.

'What's your taste in music?' she asked as she replaced the sherry bottle.

'Anything,' he said truthfully. 'I like all music—funny really, at school it was all pop and punk but when I was off work, at home, before joining the Force, I got listening to all sorts. There was nothing much to do at home, sitting around all day, and I enjoyed it all. On the radio, that is.'

'Light music then? Something from one of the shows?'

'Nice,' he said, sipping more of the sherry.

She selected a disc from her collection

and placed it on her music centre. 'Jesus Christ, Super Star,' she said. 'It's good. Very sexy.'

'It's a nice house, you keep it looking good,' he changed the subject.

'I've nothing else to spend my money on,' she was clearly pleased at his remarks. 'I'm earning good money now, what with allowances and the bits of overtime we get. Would you like a look around? There's time before we eat.'

'Thanks.' It was certainly better furnished than his parents' home, but Dad had never earned much, he'd never been paid big money. All Dad's furniture was battered and second-hand, with a distinct lack of colour sense. Not this place. The colours were all subdued, pastel shades of all kinds with mushroom browns, delicate greens, golds and yellows. She had nice wallpaper with clean paint. He wondered what his dad would think if he saw him now, sipping sherry.

She was saying, 'This is the kitchen. I

fitted those units myself with a little help from some of the lads. They're good, the lads of "B" Section. They'll always come and help their mates. Always. I got that kitchen table from an antique shop in York—it's genuine oak. Outside there's a little garden and a loo.'

She led him into the dining-room, neatly furnished in teak of a light modern style. The table was set for two with a candle burning in the centre and a bottle of red wine already opened. It looked like a posh restaurant. 'Very nice,' he murmured. 'Very nice.' God! He hadn't expected this—in his world, supper was a slice of apple pie and a cup of tea. She'd meant that about steak and Beaujolais.

'Upstairs,' she was already climbing the first steps, 'there's a bathroom and toilet, separate. Two bedrooms. I keep a second one for visitors—my mother comes sometimes and I've a sister in Manchester who likes to get away from her three kids from time to time.'

Her own bedroom, with its silk covered double bed was gorgeous, utterly feminine and laced with mirrors, curtains and thick carpets. It was another showpiece, a work of art. He thought of his bedroom at home, so sparsely fitted with a second-hand bed and a chipped, varnished wardrobe. Ma Binns wasn't much better.

'Like it?' she came close to him and he caught another whiff of her strong perfume.

'Fabulous,' was all he could say before she showed him the tiny spare room with its single bed, and the scented bathroom in case he needed it.

'It's all mine,' she was clearly proud. 'Now, time to eat. I've made a thick vegetable soup for starters, with a sirloin steak to follow. You like steak?'

'I love it,' he said, thinking of his mother's stews at mid-day with apple pie and cheese for supper. Tea was something like spaghetti on toast or beefburgers.

For Steve, it was the meal of a lifetime.

The steak was flavoured with a hot sauce of some kind which included peppers and tiny bits of red stuff, and her vegetables were superb. They drank all the wine, and the sweet was a mixed fruit salad. Afterwards they took the coffee to her settee, with Rowntrees After-Eights in a tiny dish. It had taken nearly an hour and a half to complete the meal and now she produced two glasses of brandy.

He felt euphoric. He felt utterly content and very happy. The food, the atmosphere, her chattering, the drinks, her questions about his home life and his past, the brief discussions about 'B' Section and their work—all had mingled to carry him into a sense of complete satisfaction.

'Barbara, that was marvellous. I've never had a meal like it ...'

'There's plenty more where it came from,' she settled on the sofa at his side, wafting oceans of perfume towards him. He had lost his nervousness now. 'I like company, you see. I like entertaining.

I like policemen, especially those on "B" Section.'

'I'm so new, I'm not sure how I fit in ...'

'So far, so good. Eight Oh One was delighted with the way you handled that broken window—I know he got the commendation, but it was due to your initial efforts. He'll always be grateful.'

She kicked off her red shoes and he noticed her stockings or tights were black, which made him wonder if she wore black underwear. Maybe she wore red underneath, to match her shoes?

'That's better,' she curled up on the settee at his side, clutching her brandy glass and smiling at him. One bare foot disappeared somewhere beneath her ample figure, and the other dangled over the edge of the settee. 'I do like to curl up with my shoes off. A nice fire in the grate, a good meal inside me and good company. I like you, Steve. You're not like all the others.'

'Aren't I?' What did she mean?

'You're so fresh and interesting. You've never had a meal like this?'

'No,' he admitted. 'My mum and dad can't afford to go out to cafés or hotels, so I've never been to nice places. Not like this—mum never cooks posh meals ...'

'Posh? This isn't posh, Steve! This is just a meal—a nice meal for friends. I'm not posh. I'm just a bloody policewoman, you can't get further away from being posh.'

'Maybe that's not the right word then. I mean, we never made a fuss about eating—no sherry, no wine. I mean, for our evening meal, we'd have beans on toast and apple pie. At six o'clock. For supper, there'd be a piece of tea-cake with some cheese and a cup of tea. None of this ...'

'I don't eat like this every night,' she smiled with her eyes. 'It's just when I have friends in. Sometimes I might run a big party for the Section, and sometimes there'll just be me and a friend. If I'm alone, I'll probably make do with a cheese sandwich or a piece of fruit cake.'

'But I ... I mean, well, Ma Binns couldn't do a meal like this, could she? She couldn't, Barbara, it's not her scene.'

'You approve then?'

'Approve? Of course I approve. It's great, honest. I've never had such a meal.'

'Then you'll come again?'

She eased closer now, those dark eyes smiling at him and he could see the mascara and powder; at this range, her make-up was evident but she looked great.

'I'd love to,' he heard himself saying. She stood up and shook the creases from her dress. 'More brandy?'

'I've never had brandy before,' he said.

'I like a liqueur after a meal, it just finishes it off. I'll have a Drambuie now.'

She moved gracefully to the cabinet in the far corner of the living room and poured a second rounded glass for him and a tiny glass of Drambuie for herself.

She returned to the settee and handed

both glasses to Steve while she re-arranged herself close to him. By the time she had settled, she was touching him. Her leg was nestling against his and she placed her left arm along the back of the settee, taking her tiny drink with her other hand.

'Cheers,' she raised the glass and sipped. He did likewise, the hot brandy stinging his lips. It was good, so very good.

'Cheers,' and he suddenly said. 'Here's to "B" Section—and Barbara.'

'To us, you mean,' she added, coyly.

Here it comes, he thought. He found himself quivering with suppressed nervousness as she pressed herself towards him, her eyes never leaving his face and the scent of her perfume completely embracing him.

The music was playing; she must have put on another record, but he hadn't noticed. It was gently invading the background, a long piece of soft piano music which suggested romance in the glow of the fireside, whose brightness played across the rug and the carpet, sometimes lighting her bare foot.

After a long silence, she sighed and lowered her head until it rested on his shoulder, her left arm now caressing his back. For some inexplicable reason, he shivered, and hoped his involuntary movement wouldn't break the magic of these moments.

'You're not cold?' she whispered from that position.

'No,' he said. God what should he do now. Her hair brushed his face and it was scented too. Delicate and wispy, it teased his face.

Suddenly, she sat bolt upright. The magic evaporated.

'You're nervous! You are, aren't you? You're nervous of me ...' those eyes were laughing. 'You're nervous and that's why you're shivering.'

'I am!' he laughed. 'You're dead right, Barbara. I'm terrified ...'

'Then relax, young man,' and she kissed him on the cheek. 'Just stay there and relax. The music will go on for a long time, and that brandy will warm you through. I'm warm and cosy ...'

She was. He could feel the warmth of her body against his, the movements of her legs and arms, the gentle motion of her head as she allowed her hair to embrace his face once more.

'Happy?' she asked.

'Mmm,' he said. He wondered what he was supposed to do. Maybe she would give some hint, some idea? Was he supposed to kiss her? Touch her? Just talk?'

'You're very quiet,' she said, talking to his knees.

'I'm thinking,' he said, for want of something better.

'What about?'

'You,' he replied, thinking it was a neat response.

'What about me?'

'Well, you're so bloody attractive and ...' he paused, seeking the correct word.

'Sexy?'

He laughed easily, the drink helping to make these moments easier.

'Yes, sexy. You're so sexy and bloody attractive that I can't understand why nobody's chased you and married you ...'

'Plenty have chased, but nobody's caught me,' she laughed, moving her head higher. She placed her cheek on his shoulder and smiled. 'I've not let anybody catch me because I haven't found anybody I'd like to spend the rest of my life with. I've had fun—I've had men. Lots of them, Steve. Old, young, fat and thin. Friends, acquaintances. But marriage? Not for me. I value my independence.'

'Don't you get lonely, all by yourself?'

'No, never. There are times it's nice to be alone, but I can always invite people in when I want to. Like tonight. I like you, so I can invite you into my home. I can invite who I want and when I want, and tonight, I wanted you.'

He wondered what she really meant by those final words, but her head relaxed again and he shifted his position. He extended his arm and placed it about her shoulders and this made her change position until she was relaxing in his arms with her head against the back of the settee. Suddenly, he kissed her. He kissed her full on the lips and she smiled.

'Thanks,' she said without responding, then quite rapidly, she turned and kissed him. Both arms wrapped themselves around his slender body as she pressed herself to him, her full breasts taut against her dress as she fiercely kissed his lips, then his face, chin and cheeks.

In a trice, she had changed positions. She moved until she was lying on her back, with her head in his lap, gazing up at him. The black dress exposed her upper chest, barely covering her ample breasts as she lay smiling into his eyes, with her knees raised and her bare feet on the arm of the settee.

Without speaking, she took his right hand, rubbed it with her own to make sure it was warm, then placed it on the bare expanse of flesh between her breasts. He felt himself growing strong beneath her; she must know. She must sense his reaction. She would know its effect on a young man.

He began to move his hand, instinctively exploring beneath the red trimmed edge of the black dress, pushing it aside as he began his exploration. He found there was no brassiere, nothing. He located her nipple, erect and neat on its soft base and began to move his hand, finding the right movements, the right pressure, the right timing. She began to moan gently and closed her eyes, and it was only then that he realised the dress had no buttons or fasteners down the front. A wide red belt held it closed about her waist but the skirt was simply a long length of black cloth folded over another length, and held in place by its own weight.

He moved his hand to that belt; she helped him loosen it and the dress fell completely open, aided by her moving knee.

There was nothing beneath, except black stockings on a red suspender belt and a pair of tiny pants, coloured black and red. And her waiting body. His hand moved along her smooth scented skin and she did not resist.

TEN

'Templeton's gone sick,' Sergeant Wilde informed Steve at five minutes to six one morning. 'I'm fully committed today, so you'll have to patrol alone. Can you cope?'

Steve felt a nervous twitch in his stomach. He'd never done duty alone, not completely, but now the time had come. It meant eight hours out there in a police uniform and answerable to all sections of the public and to senior officers, for all kinds of events large and small.

'Well?' Wilde was regarding him quizzically. 'Look, if you feel it's beyond you, we can put you in the office.'

'No, sergeant, no. I'd love to try alone,' he couldn't opt out of this challenge.

'How long have you been with us now?'

'Three months and a bit, sergeant.'

'You know your way around?'

'Yes, of course.'

'City centre? How about that? If I put you on City Centre patrol this morning, you think you can manage? There's not a lot to worry about—traffic problems here and there, old ladies losing cats and handbags, old men getting too much meths and falling in the gutters, kids wanting to know the history of the castle, that sort of thing.'

'Yes, I've done City Centre with TC, sarge.'

'Right. Off you go. Foot patrol with a radio. Work until ten o'clock, then come in for breakfast. If the situation's eased, we might find a panda car for you to join up with. As things are, I've Eight Oh One off sick, Five Seven Five and Six Oh One off duty because of overtime, Two Oh Seven away on a C.I.D course and Eight Eight One at court in Wolverhampton. It's left us thin on the ground, son. Look, if you've any aggro or trouble, call us up on the PR and I'll rush to your aid, like Sir Galahad.'

'I'll be fine, sergeant, honest,' Steve was looking forward to this. It would make him feel like a real policeman, just like Barbara had. She was working Juvenile Court this morning, and was scheduled to come on at nine. He wondered if she'd wake up in time—it had been one helluva night last night. She was dynamite, sheer bloody dynamite and utterly insatiable ... but he could cope. He was a man all right.

He collected his PR and tested the batteries. Everything was in working order and its signal was loud and clear, so he tucked the set down his tunic, fastened the strong clip over the lapels and felt confident. The radio gave him confidence. This link with Control was his life-line; without it, he felt naked and helpless, rather like a baby must feel when its umbilical cord was severed during those first vital moments of life. It must be tough, being a baby, having to survive all the hazards of birth and depending all the time on other people for your very existence.

They'd taught him all about childbirth at Training School, just in case he had to deal with a pregnant mum who was trying to be pregnant no longer. Many young officers had encountered pregnant women giving birth during their first tours of duty, either in houses, shops, ambulances and even in the street. During the lectures he hadn't thought he could cope with the embarrassment of seeing a strange woman so naked down there ... but he'd seen Barbara now, many times. Now, he could cope. She was thick with dark hair, all filled out with smooth white flesh. Had she ever had a baby? She was thirty-five, she'd really told him, and someone said that you should never trust a woman who told you her age. If she'd tell you that, she'd tell you anything.

'Right,' Sergeant Wilde's voice roused him from his day-dreaming. 'To your beats, everybody. One reminder—look out for those con men. They've called on several old ladies on the outskirts in recent weeks, pretending to be collecting odds and ends for charity. There's no charity—they get inside the houses, see what's there and call back weeks later to break in. Warn your public, lads. Keep an eye on old folks. Some have been forcibly burgled, remember. Twelve Fifteen, call on a few shops in town and warn them too. Ask 'em to tell their regular customers about villains—you know, newspaper shops, the bakers and butchers. Get 'em to pass the word around.'

'Yes, sergeant,' they chorused as they moved towards the exit.

Kev caught up with Steve as they moved from One Box. 'You made it, then?'

Steve smiled. 'I was on time,' he answered with a knowing smile.

'You shouldn't shack up with her, you

know. Do the bosses know?'

'It's my private life, Kev!'

'You've no private life in this job, mate. I've told you that. Look Steve, I'm your pal. Leave her alone. Get out.'

'It was just last night—and I was on earlies.'

'She wasn't. She's not on till nine. She'll drain you dry, Steve. She's ravenous.'

'I know,' Steve smiled knowingly. 'She's good ...'

'She wants young lads like you. She's too fit for blokes of her own age. She likes young blood, keen lads who'll manage it time and time again through the night ...'

'So I'm good, I know that now.'

'And you, the section virgin!'

'She's a good teacher, and I'm a willing pupil. Look, Kev, I've no intention of moving in with her, I'm not daft. I'll stay the odd night, no more. I'm learning, I want to learn. I want to grow up; I'm a fully blown copper, Kev, and I'm only eighteen! I don't want to go around not knowing about life, not having to do a job like this.'

'You're still on probation, remember. Two years' probation lies ahead of you and if for any reason they think you're not likely to make an efficient police officer, they can sack you. There's no appeal. Nothing. You're out.'

'Does our private life come into that, then?'

'You bet it does, Steve. If they know you're shacking up with the Section Bike, they'll mark your cards.'

'Do they know? Sands I mean? Or the sergeants?'

'They make it their business to know, Steve. Honest, it's not worth the risk if you value the job.'

'But outside, solicitors, barristers, top business men—they all sleep with women, they all shack up and sleep over the brush ... why can't we?'

'When you've got your two years in, it

doesn't matter. They can't touch you then, although it might mean you're held back for promotion. But they can't sack you for sleeping over the brush, not after your probation's over.'

'I'm not sleeping over the brush!'

'You slept there last night, and other nights. We covered for you with Ma Binns, said you'd had to go home on family business. She might raise the alarm—she worries if we're out late. She's worse than a mother.'

'I'll tell her I had to see my dad about something personal.'

'You do, but don't forget she knows you're not friends with your dad. Right, here we are, the parting of the ways.'

They were outside the station now and Kev moved towards a waiting panda car. 'What time are you mealing?'

'Ten.'

'Me too. See you in Ma Binns then?'

'Er ...'

'Not Barbara's surely?'

'No. I thought I might eat in the canteen this morning.'

'Balls, Barbara will be bringing you a plate of Kellogg's and a slice of toast into the policewomen's room, eh? Before she goes into court—you'll have a quick jump while she's reading the files and you're gnawing your toast.'

'Balls, Kevin! She said she'd have coffee in the canteen before she goes into court ...'

'Oh bloody hell, you've got it bad. O.K. I'll tell Ma Binns you're in the canteen. What about your dinner after shift?'

'I'll be there,' Steve promised.

'Because your lady friend's on all day and won't be in till five?'

'She's going home after five. She has to see her father.'

'Or another fit feller, maybe? Is somebody doing a bit for her at her parent's place as well? Home's Huddersfield, isn't it? See you,' and Kev walked towards the car. Steve watched him walk with an air of confidence, with the style of a man accustomed to wearing uniform and a man completely satisfied with his own rôle in society. Kev was good for him, he decided.

'Drive carefully,' Steve called for want of something to say, and turned out of the station gates to walk to the City centre. It was quarter past six on a bright spring morning.

On his way into the centre of the quiet morning town, he felt assured and proud to wear the uniform. He was no longer afraid of the unexpected. He thought of his father's reaction when he'd broken the news, of his antagonism towards the police, his hatred of anything that represented the Establishment, of wealthy people, of private education, of success in life ...

Yet here he was, striding into one of Britain's major cities with all the assurance of a mature constable. Certainly, Barbara had helped; her ministrations over the past few weeks had boosted his ego and he felt a glow of confidence as his long strides took him closer to the morning's beat.

Several people wished him good morning. This was a significant aspect of police work—the early morning workers always spoke and were always smiling and happy. Not like the night when they came out of the pubs feeling belligerent, aggressive and wanting to fight everybody. The mornings were lovely—the postmen, the early morning council workers, the men who staffed the lemonade factory, the window cleaners, bus drivers, railway workers ... they all smiled and bade him good morning. Schoolboys carrying huge loads of newspapers on bicycles smiled too. He decided he liked mornings.

Why did darkness and drink change it all? Could it be an ancient, inherited fear of the dark? Was darkness a threat? Stephen Crosby found himself philosophising about life and human behaviour; he found himself looking at people in a way he'd never considered before. He saw them in black and white categories—so good and happy on the one hand and so appallingly awful on the other. This morning, they were happy and smiling but tonight some of these carefree workers would be threatening the police or the public or one another with fists, bottles or knives. Some poor young copper would have to go and sort it out. Maybe he'd get injured for his trouble. Steve shook his head; he wished his father was walking the streets with him, not just this morning but all the time. It would shake his dad's views. Mum seemed to know how people behaved, but not dad. He thought bad behaviour was due to capitalist repression. Poor old dad, he couldn't distinguish between free enterprise and Victorian capitalism, and regarded anyone who made money as a monster.

Steve found himself thinking about politics too. Policemen had not to involve themselves with politics, which was another of the rules by which they had to live. It didn't stop them thinking about politics, but as a youngster he knew little about the difference between the political parties. Lately, though, he'd read the Daily Mirror and some of the political rubbish it printed when there was a riot and policemen were hurt. He'd read the Sunday Express at Ma Binns' house and the Daily Mail in the canteen. They all said something different and when MPs appeared on television, they never answered questions. They just said what they wanted and it all seemed so confusing. It was clear that the Socialists didn't like policemen, though. Why was that? Policemen were there to protect life and property, to detect crime and apprehend criminals, so why didn't the Socialists like them? And what about the new Social Democrats? Did they like the police? The Conservatives did; they fought for policemen's rights and conditions because policemen were there to protect the public, so the Conservatives were helping to protect citizens.

'Morning, officer,' it was a smartly dressed gentleman who spoke with an Oxford accent. 'Could you help me please? I'm looking for the road out to Middlesbrough. I've been staying overnight at the Dane Hotel and can't find my way out of this town ... I have a car, over in the Greenfields Car Park, and I must reach Middlesbrough by nine o'clock ...'

With infinite patience, Steve directed the man from the car park and out onto the major road which skirted the town before leading north into Middlesbrough's grime and depression. The man thanked him profusely.

It was seven thirty. Several church clocks struck and the city was growing increasingly busy. People were on the streets, cars and buses were filling the atmosphere with fumes and noise, cyclists were weaving between them, getting to the front at the traffic lights and shouting to one another as they all rushed somewhere. Where were they all going? Why? Lots of them were schoolchildren—at this early hour?

His patrolling occupied him until nine o'clock by which time the town was humming with activity. He found it so exhilarating—people came up and asked directions and sought his advice. He found himself giving them his opinions on the best places to get coffee, the best shops for three-piece suites, the finest hotels, the best sight-seeing tours. Lots of Americans asked him to pose with friends for photographs and promised to send him copies when they were printed, back in the States. They took his address and said they'd send copies to him as a form of gratitude.

Quite suddenly, it was time to head back to the station for his meal break. The time had flown. In the canteen, Barbara was drinking her coffee with the rest of the section and he joined them after ordering bacon and eggs. His feet were aching and his throat thirsting for a hot drink; the fumes of the traffic had dried him drastically, and when he sat down next to

Barbara she pressed her thigh against his and he forgot about his thirst for coffee. He began to thirst after her ...

She chattered amiably to the others with her thigh pressed against his all the time, and he tackled his breakfast with a gusto that surprised him. Normally, he didn't feel like eating but this morning's early outing with its exercise and exhilarating contact with human life had combined to provoke a healthy appetite.

'Ring me,' Barbara said as she left to collect her files for court. 'I'm back tonight, for earlies tomorrow.'

'Sure,' and he watched her leave the table. She was not particularly attractive in uniform. The shapeless clothing concealed her fine figure and the heavy police skirt made her look positively matronly. But underneath, there were the black stockings and that tiny patch of red which she called her panties. If only the magistrates knew—he smiled at the thought. The Chairman would blow a gasket!

Sergeant Wilde joined them at the table. 'Hello, Twelve Fifteen. This is an honour. Is Ma Binns having a day off?'

'I went home last night, sarge, and forgot to remind her I'd be back for breakfast, so I thought I'd eat here. Nice grub, eh?'

'It's better than a lot of that mush they sell to the tourists out there.' He chomped a large sausage with obvious relish. 'And cheaper.'

Steve tucked in too. He was thoroughly enjoying the good-natured banter around him, and the happy chatter of his section mates. Half of those on duty had come in now, the other half having eaten at nine o'clock. Some were playing cards, and one was deep into Page Three of the Sun. Some of the office staff were in for coffee and biscuits, and a Chief Inspector strolled across and queued for a coffee. That wouldn't happen at Training School—Chief Inspectors were privileged there, and never queued for anything.

'Any problems this morning, Twelve Fifteen?'

'Nothing, sergeant. All went very smoothly.'

'There'd be questions all the time, eh? How where and when. Tourists and shoppers. Where's the best car park, mister? How can I find the Railway Station? What time's the next train to Glasgow? That sort of stuff.'

'It helped me get used to the uniform and being alone, sergeant.'

'So you fancy another crack at it after meal break?'

'Please.'

'O.K. You're on your tod.'

And so, for the second half of his shift, he was alone once more. He strode steadfastly back to his beat, smiling at people and bidding them good morning. In the town centre, he resumed his patrol, walking along the outer edge of the footpaths as he had been advised at Training School. There he could be seen and the deterrent value of his uniform provided its best advantage; furthermore, he was in a position to dash to any incident, large or small, instead of being hemmed in by crowds or lost behind shop façades and other protrusions.

It was during this second half of his patrol that he decided to enter shops and spread the gospel of the villains who were preying on old folks. One problem was that the shops were all busy; the people behind the counters were constantly under pressure and few had time to talk at any length. Surprisingly, many of them waved him through to their small room at the back. There, a girl assistant would rush in, make him a coffee and rush back to the customers. In some, he found himself chatting to the girls if they had time, or to the shop owners or managers. He managed to put forward his message when he remembered, but on more than one occasion, he found himself chatting up the shop assistants in the quieter shops, and completely forgetting about his mission.

There was a fascinating girl in the dry cleaners', for example. He had entered that place because lots of ladies came here with their garments and he felt he could pass on the message about the thieves. The place wasn't busy—far from it and the girl smiled as he entered.

'You're new, aren't you?' she said.

'Yes, it's my first time,' he told her. 'I'm under instruction really, but we're short handed, so I'm on my own.'

She listened to his tale about the rogues and promised to tell all her old-age customers. Then she asked, 'Would you like a coffee? There's one behind the counter, round that screen.'

'Thanks.' He was full of coffee but she was lovely. He'd drink anything just to be with her for a few minutes longer.

He went behind the screen and there was a small enclosed area with two chairs and a rough table. It bore a kettle, milk, coffee and mugs. He switched on the kettle and she came to join him.

'I can hear the bell go when customers come in,' she said. 'I'll make it for us.'

He watched as she busied herself with the coffees.

'You're alone too?' he said by way of opening the conversation.

'It's Tuesday, it's always quiet on Tuesdays,' she said, 'so our manageress takes her day off. I have Saturdays off.'

'Do you live in Pollsfield?' he asked.

She poured hot water into the mugs and smiled. 'Yes, out on the Cransfield Road. It's a little side street called Shoe Street. It used to be full of cobblers' shops years ago, so they say.'

'I don't know it, but I know Cransfield Road. Do you cycle in?'

'No, I use the bus. The Number 15. It goes right past our street and it's handy. We open nine to five-thirty, and the buses are just right. Where do you live?'

'I'm in digs here,' he said. 'We call her Ma Binns, it's in Ashford Terrace. There's four of us there.'

'All policemen?'

'Yes, all of us. We're all on the same Section, so we work the same hours.'

'It must be very interesting, being a policeman.' She passed the coffee to him and he thanked her. She was a pretty girl, with curly black hair and rounded face with a cute little nose. Her eyes were grey, he noticed, and she had a mole on her left cheek, just below the jaw line. She'd be about eighteen, he reckoned, and well built, not fat but not thin, and a nice average height. She wore a shapeless green overall so he couldn't see much of her figure, although her legs were pretty with very slim ankles.

He told her something of his job, emphasising the glamour parts and ignoring the drudgery of shift-work. She listened and he found himself wanting to know more about her.

'What's your name?' he asked.

'Elaine,' she smiled, blushing slightly. 'Elaine Stuart.'

'I'm Stephen Crosby,' he said. 'Nice to meet you, Elaine.'

'Nice to meet you,' she smiled.

'You're not married or anything?' he put to her, his confidence high.

She laughed. 'Not me! I've had boyfriends, but I haven't a steady feller, not now.'

'You've fallen out?'

'Not really, just drifted apart. I'm not worried, he was useless. A drifter, you know. Didn't have a job and never tried; couldn't get out of bed on a morning to find work.'

'I can't get out of bed either, but it's sheer idleness!' he laughed.

'But you have got a job, haven't you?' He saw the fire in her eyes. 'You've taken the trouble to get out and look for something.'

'And so have you,' he put to her.

'Yes, I did. I went right through the Yellow Pages, ringing every place in town—well, nearly every place. I asked them for a job—and I got this. I've had it a year now. It's not much, but it's a job.'

'You got "O" levels, then?'

'Yes, six. I felt I could get a better job, but this is a start. I'm going to night school, studying shorthand and typing, and when I'm qualified I'll try for an office job somewhere. Maybe something better will come—but right now, I take soiled clothes from the public and send them out looking smarter. I suppose that is useful.'

He smiled. She was a lovely girl and obviously had determination and guts.

'Look,' he heard himself say. 'What about tonight? Do you fancy a drink?'

'Oh, it's night school,' she lowered her eyes. 'I'm working for an exam, otherwise I could have given it a miss ...'

'Oh,' he felt dejected. She wasn't avoiding him, though. He knew that.

'I finish at nine,' she came back, smiling.

'All right. Shall I meet you outside at nine, and we'll pop into a quiet place for a drink?'

'I'd like that,' she said. 'Yes, I would. Where shall I meet you?'

'Where's your night school?'

'It's at Mansion House Comprehensive.'

'All right, see you there. I haven't a car, mind.'

'Me neither. There's a nice pub nearby, the Golden Calf.'

'Nine o'clock it is,' he said. 'Thanks for the coffee, Elaine.'

The shop bell rang and she made her excuse to leave. He sailed out feeling like a bird in the heavens; she was lovely, she was gorgeous. And he'd chatted her up very successfully. It must be the uniform; maybe she was kinky about uniforms. No, she liked him. It was as simple as that.

One of his ports of call that day was a small jeweller's shop just off the main shopping thoroughfare. It was staffed by a man in middle age, balding, with half-rimmed spectacles. Steve entered commence his chatter about the risks to old folks and the jeweller listened carefully.

He made notes on a pad on the counter and quizzed the policeman closely about the finer points of the illegality of their actions and methods of operating. Steve was able to satisfy his healthy curiosity.

When Steve had finished, the man said, 'You know, officer, you are the first uniformed policeman I've had in my shop for several weeks. Once, we got them all in, giving us lists of stolen property, advice about shoplifters or burglars, but now they flash past in their cars. They haven't got time to call.'

Steve explained how the new policy was to walk about on foot patrols and told the interested jeweller of the new ideals. He listened with evident interest and then said,

'Wait a moment.'

He went into a side room and returned with a large brooch. It was a pale blue colour, clearly a stone of some kind, and it was set in a circle of gold coloured ornaments, each with a pale blue eye in the centre.

'See this?'

'Yes?'

'It was brought in by a woman who cleans at the Royal Hotel. She's a skivvy, a maid, not the sort of person to have this kind of jewellery. It's not the first piece she's brought in, officer; this item is worth well over £150 by my reckoning. She says she had them left by a maiden aunt, and is selling them to raise money because her husband is on the dole.'

'And you don't believe her?'

'I'm not happy about it. She doesn't seem the sort of woman who would have this kind of jewellery.'

'Not even if it was left by a maiden aunt?' put in Steve.

'Who can say? I've been in this business a long time, officer, and I've a feeling about that woman.'

'Does she work there full time?'

'I don't know. I did wonder if she was

stealing jewellery from residents.'

'I think we would have known,' Steve felt some thefts would have been reported.

'Maybe not, young man. Lots of elderly women don't really know what they're carrying or where they put things.'

'Look,' said Steve. 'I'll check with our C.I.D. Maybe they have been told of a sneak thief at the Crown. Will you keep the things here for a while?'

'Yes, there's this brooch and a bracelet in solid silver. The bracelet is excellent. She brought the bracelet in, oh, six weeks ago, and the brooch about a week since.'

'You've not sold them?'

'No, I wasn't happy about them. I didn't feel like wasting police time by bringing your men in especially, but now you're here ...'

'Keep them in your drawer, Mr ...?'

'Lamb.'

'Mr Lamb. I'll ask among the C.I.D and will let you know what happens. Do you know the woman's name?'

'She said it was Mrs Ireland.'

'Thanks,' Steve's heart fluttered with an inexplicable excitement. 'I'll look into this for you.'

ELEVEN

He went to Ma Binns' after duty, had lunch and shaved away the growth of the early morning. He followed with a quick bath in beautifully hot and soapy water which washed away the perspiration and female smells of the last night. Tonight he was going to be with Elaine, and he wanted to be clean for her. By the time he had finished his washing and cleaning, it was after three o'clock; tea was at five thirty and Elaine didn't finish night school until nine.

The lads were in their rooms too, putting up their feet after a long morning shift and he decided to see what Kev was doing this afternoon. He knocked on his door and was invited in.

'Hello, Twelve Fifteen. Staying in then?'

'Yes, why?'

'I thought you must have moved in with Barbara,' he laughed. 'She must have given you a night to remember.'

Stephen blushed. 'She did.'

'You're not the first, she eats young constables. She'll wear you out, mate, believe me. I've told you enough times.'

'What a way to go!' Steve sat on the bed beside his pal. 'Have you been there?'

'Not me. I'm fussy. I like to pursue a woman, you know—the hunting instinct of the male and all that. I don't like 'em to present it to me on a plate.'

'She's worked hard for me, Kev. Nice meal, music, wine—the full honours. It was great, and I thoroughly enjoyed it.'

'And tonight? It'll be a repeat performance tonight, then?'

'Tonight. No, well, you see I chatted up this bird in a cleaner's down town, Elaine. She's nice. I'm seeing her tonight, after night classes.'

'What about Barbara then?'

'She's got her own life ... bloody hell! I forgot! I said I'd ring her after duty ... she's going home, to her parents.'

'She'll have you round there for another session, believe me.'

'No, she won't be back till late. I'm seeing Elaine anyway.'

'Then you'd better have a good excuse if Barbara does come back early—say you've had to go home because your mum wanted to wash your underpants or something.'

'You'll cover for me?'

'Sure. We don't reckon much to the Station Bike anyway. You like this Elaine?'

Steve nodded. 'She's nice. Pure, I reckon. Nice, real nice.'

'Drop Barbara then. She'll raise hell and accuse you of using her body but you're as well rid, Steve. Now, what's on this afternoon?'

'That's why I came down to see you. I've nothing to do.'

'Me neither. Fancy a game of snooker?'

'It's years since I played. We've a table

in the village hall, but I never got up there much.'

'We'll go down to the nick. There's three tables in the club. I'll teach you.'

'Thank you.'

They walked to the station and found an empty table, where Kev showed as much skill with snooker balls as he did with a football. He was a natural ball player and patient with it. In no time, he was explaining the finer points of the game to young Steve, and Steve found himself enjoying the experience. They talked shop all the time; Kev told him of today's work, of the traffic accident he'd dealt with, of the old lady who'd lost her purse and of the crowds outside a record shop in town, where Abba had been autographing records.

'How about you, Steve? Did you have a good day? It was your first solo flight, wasn't it?'

'Yes, I enjoyed it,' and he went through the day, spending a lot of time talking about Elaine, but omitting to mention Mr Lamb and the suspected stolen goods. He thought it wise not to mention this to anyone; if he could deal with the case himself, he might get praise and eventual attachment to C.I.D. He hadn't forgotten TC's unearned commendation.

And so the afternoon was pleasantly occupied to be followed by one of Ma Binns' superb teas. By six o'clock, he was ready to leave but there was another three hours before he could meet Elaine. Should he ring Barbara? She said something about coming home later tonight, in time for early turn, so she'd be out now. He could meet Elaine at nine, take her out for a drink and then go back to Barbara's ...

He lay on his bed, thinking about them. Barbara had done him a world of good and had made him feel like a man. But if all they said was true, she wouldn't want him for what he was. She'd want him for his ability as a stallion, for sex, nothing but sex. But he liked the meal, the treatment, and the sex. He'd needed Barbara's skills.

Elaine, young, beautiful, innocent. A nice girl. One you could marry. You'd never marry Barbara, not a woman like that who'd been around with every Tom, Dick and Harry in town. She'd be like a second-hand bike. But even so, he wanted her, he felt himself aching for her, he felt himself wanting her right now. He was responding even now to memories of her last night, in that dress, out of those pants, that tuft of black hair, the movements of her body beneath him, above him, about him.

He got off the bed and walked around the room, pacing up and down in the confined space, all the time wanting another session with that superb teacher but at the same time wanting to know more about the pure Elaine. He longed to be with her, all alone and just talking, finding out about each other in the nicest possible way.

He went downstairs to the lounge. Brew

Ten was watching television and he settled into an arm chair at his side. Brew Ten acknowledged his arrival with a nod and resumed his viewing. He reminded Steve of his dad, just sitting there, gaping at the screen.

Kev had gone out, Ma Binns said, and so had Martin, to some disco. They'd told her about Steve and his new girl, explaining that's why they hadn't invited him along. They hadn't wished to place him in the dilemma of deciding whether to have a night out with his pals or a date with a girl he hardly knew.

Finally, half past eight arrived and he left Ma Binns and Brew Ten to their television viewing and caught a bus to Mansion House Comprehensive School. It was ten minutes to nine when he arrived and he could see the lights in the building, with busy people bowed over desks and teachers pacing backwards and forwards before their classes. It wouldn't be a bad idea to attend night school, he reasoned;

after all, he'd neglected school. He might learn a language, or do art. They'd have laughed at him at school, talking like that. Art! That was for cissies ...

At the stroke of nine, people rushed out of the classrooms for buses and cars, or pedalled cycles down the long drive to the main road. He waited near the bus shelter, his eyes peeled for Elaine and for one horrible moment, he wondered if he would recognise her. Would she know him, now he was out of uniform?

His anxious eyes scanned the quick crowd and then he saw her. She was walking with another girl about her own age, a slender girl with fair hair and they seemed to be pals. She was looking for him. He knew that. He watched them approach the end of the drive and waved at her. She didn't see him.

She was standing at the exit, talking distantly to her friend so he waved again, and shouted this time. 'Hello, Elaine!'

She saw him and her eyes lit up. He

crossed the busy road, running to dodge the oncoming traffic and presented himself to her.

'Hello,' he said. 'You made it.'

'Yes, and you? You got finished all right?'

'Yes, bang on time.'

'Oh, this is Sue. She's an old school friend, and we go to night classes together. Sue, this is Steve.'

'Hi, Steve. Well, I mustn't play gooseberry. I'm supposed to be meeting Alan now.'

'Alan works in a bank,' Elaine explained. 'They've been going steady for nine months now.'

'Is he picking you up here?' Steve asked.

'Yes, but he's always late. He always manages to get his head buried in a television programme and forgets about me until it ends. Ah, talk of the devil!'

A small ancient red mini-car was chugging towards them, and it pulled into the area close to the open school gates. A tall, smiling youth with neat hair and a tartan shirt climbed out, having apparently been curled up inside the tiny vehicle. How on earth he squeezed his long frame in there, Steve would never know.

'Hi,' he shouted, beaming all over. 'Am I late again? I left when the ads came on, Sue, honest.'

'Alan, this is Steve He's Elaine's friend.'

'Hi, Steve. Nice to meet you. Well, what's on tonight?'

He looked at them all, first at Steve and Elaine, then at his own girl, wondering whether he should play gooseberry or be a taxi-driver.

'I was going to take Elaine for a drink—the Golden Calf, isn't it?'

'Mind if we come then?' Sue asked. 'We can ride in Esmerelda.'

'Smashing,' Alan beamed. 'Pile in, folks. Never mind the springs.'

And so they all adjourned to the lovely olde worlde inn. Alan and Sue proved to be marvellous company, full of fun and bright ideas, always looking for places to go, new experiences to enjoy and new worlds to conquer. They asked Steve all about himself, about his job and prospects and he found himself liking them very much. Alan's background was so different from his own—Alan's father was a solicitor with a big practice in Leeds, but Alan had opted for his career away from his father's profession. He had a flat in Pollsfield which he shared with another pal, also a bank employee. Sue was his girl—she worked in a Mail Order firm's headquarters on the outskirts, looking after invoices and accounts.

After a couple of drinks, Alan said, 'Well, Steve, we've been in your way long enough. Sue, old girl, come along. We'll vanish and leave these two to find out more about each other. Look, Steve, join us again. I'm in Barclay's in town—leave messages, call in. I'm usually around.'

'Thanks. Bye, Sue. Bye Alan.'

They watched them leave and Steve turned to Elaine.

'They're nice,' he said, meaning every word. 'They're very nice.'

'Yes, I like them. Sue's always been a close friend and well, Alan's just great. He could have lived off his dad, but didn't want to. He left home to fend for himself, and he's studying for his banking exams. He wants to specialise in something foreign—I'm not sure what, but I think it's to do with the exchange rate.'

'How did the class go?' he asked.

'Not bad. I learned a bit more, for the exams. I must pass them, Steve, I don't want to be stuck behind that counter all my life.'

'You won't be, I'm sure. And I don't want to spend all my days plodding the streets fighting with yobbos. There are some good jobs in the police service, specialist jobs and interesting work. I'm going to do my best to pass all my exams as well.'

'I'm sure you will. What happened today? Anything exciting? It must be exciting, working as a policeman.'

'You never know what's going to happen next,' he laughed, and he found himself telling her about the jewellery and the suspected thief at the Crown Hotel.

'Just think,' she said when he'd finished, 'you might arrest an international jewel thief!'

'More like some poor woman who's hard up and pinching the stuff to make ends meet!'

'What will you do?'

'I was going to make my own enquiries into it,' he said. 'People in the job keep saying I mustn't tell C.I.D because they'll take the case off me and get all the praise. My Tutor Constable did that ...'

He explained all about the rôle of his tutor constable, and the arrest of Simpson with the stolen television sets. She sympathised with him but reminded him that he was still under instruction.

He couldn't rush things, he must learn steadily.

'Yes, I suppose you're right. At home, they wouldn't give a complicated electrician's job to a new lad, would they? He'd stand by and watch.'

'That would be for his own safety, Steve. I think you should go by the book. Tell somebody.'

'I'd like to get into C.I.D. Maybe I should tell the detective inspector?'

'I would. At your stage in service, you mustn't go about taking big jobs off the professionals, must you? Suppose it all went wrong.'

He thought about it. Her advice was so sensible. Yes, he would pass on the gen to the C.I.D.

They talked about her, about her family and her ambitions. She was a quiet girl, he realised, not too fond of bright lights and night clubs, but preferring to walk in the countryside or visit historic places like ruined abbeys, castles and so forth. She found it difficult, not having a car, for her previous boy had had a car, but hated such places. He was all for pubs and darts and discos and football matches.

'I don't drive,' Steve confessed, 'but they'll be sending me on a driving course soon. Every policeman has to go on the course, they teach us up to the police standard, and then I'll buy a little car.'

'We could go all over!' she enthused, and from that remark he knew she liked him. After their drinks, he walked her home, idling on the way and stopping to window-shop, to look at the sights of the city at night, to talk about their future, his shifts and his weekends on duty.

Eventually, they reached her home, a neat semi-detached house in a pleasant street. She stopped at the gate.

'Will I see you again?' he asked.

'I'd like that, Steve.'

'I'm on day off the next two days. You'll be at work?'

' 'Fraid so.'

'Evenings, then? We'll go somewhere.'

'There's a mystery tour tomorrow evening,' she told him. 'It's a bus leaving the Museum at seven thirty, and touring the Yorkshire Dales, calling at a pub somewhere for a bar snack. How about that?'

'Do you want to go?'

She nodded. 'I'd love to,' she said. 'Alan and Sue are going—I wasn't, because I was alone, but if you ...'

'Consider it done,' he smiled. 'Where shall I see you?'

'Outside the Museum, quarter to seven?'

'I'll be there,' and he kissed her quickly. She responded equally quickly, kissing him full on the mouth before retreating along the path to the front door. He blew a kiss as she opened the door and said, 'Tomorrow, then?'

'Tomorrow,' and he walked away elated beyond all his dreams.

He decided to walk home to Ma Binns'. Most of the lads went home on their rest days, instead of remaining in digs, but dad didn't make his trips home very welcoming. He thought Steve was spying, so he preferred to keep out of the way. He spent a lot of time in the digs, spending the mornings in bed and the afternoons with the lads, but now ...

With a spring in his step, he began to walk the mile or so back to Ma Binns', whistling happily and striding along with a definite jauntiness. This was the life. He had freedom, a girl friend of extraordinary charm, no nagging mother to ask where he'd been, and money in his pocket.

And then he realised he was passing the police station. The lights were shining from most of the windows as befits a building open 24 hours per day. People were busy in the offices. He remembered Elaine's words, her eminently sensible words, and on impulse decided to call in and talk to a C.I.D man. After all, he was off duty for the coming two days and the story would lose something by delay. They could even miss the thief.

He pushed open the front door and entered.

TWELVE

'Is there anyone in C.I.D?' he asked the night constable behind the desk.

'Name?' asked the officer blandly.

'I'm P.C Crosby, I'm in the job. "B" Section.'

'Oh, the new lad, eh? Go straight up,' and the constable pressed a button at the side of the desk. This released the lock on the inner door which led to the stairs, and Steve climbed to the first floor. The door leading into the large open-plan C.I.D room stood open, and light poured out to flood the dark corridors. He peered around the door. Two or three plain-clothes men were at their desks, scribbling reports or checking files. He coughed to announce his presence and walked in.

No one took any notice of him. He stood a moment, feeling intrusive before he approached one of them. This was a big man with a mop of tight curly hair and a large ugly wart growing from his chin.

'Yes, what is it?'

'I'm Twelve Fifteen,' Steve used police jargon. ' "B" Section.'

'So?'

'I've got some information.'

'Ah. Good, is it? Reliable?'

'Yes, very.'

'Why tell me, son?' The man was about fifty and very heavily built, with a surly character.

'I'm off duty tomorrow and the day after, and was passing the nick. I thought I'd better tell somebody.'

'There's nobody better than me. I'm Archie Creaser. Sit down.'

The man did not reveal his rank, so Steve reckoned he was a constable, a D.C meaning Detective Constable. Steve pulled up a chair and settled down at his side.

'Well, son, give; what is it?'

Steve told him about Mr Lamb the jeweller and the theory about the thief at the Royal Hotel. Creaser listened intently, his pale grey eyes flickering across Steve's face all the time. He asked some very personal questions, and after fifteen minutes seemed very satisfied with Steve's account.

'Nice one, son. I like it. You haven't mentioned this to anybody else?'

'No, I came across it today before I went off duty and haven't told anybody else.'

'Not even your sergeant?'

'No, I haven't seen him to report it.'

'Not to worry, son. I'll see to it. Now, you're Crosby, eh? Steve Crosby, Twelve Fifteen of "B" Section. Leave it with me. I'll have a word with my D.I and we'll see what happens. It looks a good one. I'll be in touch.'

'Thanks, Mr Creaser.'

'Archie. They all call me Archie,' and Steve left the quiet room. Lots of the desks were empty, and he realised this would be the night shift, most of whom would be out and about in the city, doing the clubs and pubs, nosing around for titbits of information.

He felt very content now and realised it had been the best thing to do. It relieved him of responsibility, for he realised he couldn't hope to cope with a complex criminal enquiry at his stage of service. There was all the paperwork, the statistical information required, the Judges' Rules, court procedures, bail.

'Hello?' a voice said as he neared the foot of the stairs on the way out. It was Barbara, smelling like a perfume factory and looking like a thousand dollars.

'Oh, hello Barbara. Been having a night out?'

'Yes, I went home to see dad. He's fine, so I came up to the club for a late drink. And you?'

'C.I.D,' he said, wondering if she would interpret that as an explanation of some overtime job.

'Not working?'

'No, I was passing and had some gen for them. I've just been up.'

'Good stuff, was it?' she linked arms and propelled him towards the door which led into the front office. 'Crime?'

'Yes,' he said as the door opened. They were at the main entrance now and she called 'Goodnight, Reg,' to the man behind the counter.

Outside, Barbara announced that her car was in the car park and she would give him a lift. He felt inclined to refuse, knowing she'd want more than to give him a lift, but she insisted. She unlocked the door of her Fiesta and bade him sit in the passenger seat.

'You were going to ring me,' she said.

'I got involved, I've just come in. If you hadn't been there, at the nick, I'd have rung.'

'Coming home with me then?' she invited, starting the engine.

'Ma Binns is expecting me,' he countered.

'Ring her, say you won't be in. You've gone home, tell her.'

'I never go home on my days off, she knows that. My dad objects to me being a copper. Besides, all my things are in my room.'

'O.K. Be like that. I like men, Steve, not boys ... come along, I'll drop you at Ma Binns'.'

'I didn't mean that,' he began to protest. 'Sorry, I'm so unsure of myself ...'

'Then come with me, stay a couple of hours and then go to Ma Binns ...'

He didn't reply. He was thinking of Elaine.

'A cup of coffee, a quick drink to follow and, well, who knows ...' she smiled and kissed him briefly on the cheek before turning onto the road.

He felt himself responding, he felt the

tremors in his loins, the aching for her warmth and moistness, the desire to smell her and run his hands across that smooth skin.

'All right,' he said and she patted his knee.

In the cosiness of her house, Steve waited on the settee as she brewed coffee and she had told him to help himself to a drink from the sideboard. He selected a whisky, and poured a gin and tonic for Barbara.

When she emerged with two mugs of steaming coffee, she set them on the small table before the settee and plonked herself beside him, snuggling close as she reached for the coffee.

'Cosy, isn't it?' she oozed.

'Lovely.' He moved his head and quickly kissed her cheek, displaying some nervousness. 'Thanks for inviting me.'

'I thought you weren't going to come,' she said.

'I didn't think you'd want me to. I'm

not exactly a prize catch for a woman like you.'

'You're a prize catch for any woman, Steve,' and she sipped from the hot mug. 'What was that about C.I.D tonight? You've not been giving them gen, have you?'

'Yes, I thought we were supposed to.'

'They'll take all the credit, you know.'

'But we're all in the same job, Barbara, damn it all. It's all for the same end.'

'Try telling C.I.D that. They live in a world apart. What was it, this important piece of gen?'

'I was in a jeweller's today, warning them about those bastards who steal from old folks. Well, this jeweller, Lamb they call him, was so chuffed to see a uniform policeman giving advice that he told me about a woman who he thinks is nicking jewels from somewhere. He's got some of the stuff in the shop, locked away. She works at the Royal, a maid of some sort.'

'And you told C.I.D?' she cried.

'Aren't we supposed to do that?'

'You should have told your sergeant, Steve. That would have been a good crime knock-off for "B" Section. We could have raised two fingers to the rest and proved yet again that "B" is Best.'

'Would we have done the enquiry?'

'Yes, the lot. The sergeant would have helped you, you'd get the arrest if there was one, and you'd follow the crime right through, enquiries, crime reports and court. The lot. Who did you tell?'

'It was a big chap with a wart on his chin.'

'Creaser! Of all the bastards ... he'll take all the credit for that one, Steve. You'll never get a look in.'

'He said he'd contact me.'

'He will, when it's all over. Oh, poor young Steve. You've a lot to learn.'

'Sometimes I wonder if I ever will learn it all. It's all so complicated, what with divisional boundaries, C.I.D work, traffic, sudden deaths ...'

'And women,' she said, placing her mug on the table. With her warm hands, she loosened the buttons on his shirt and began to explore his body, resting her scented head upon his chest. He thought of the whisky on the table, he thought of the sergeant's anger when he returned to duty, he thought of Ma Binns and he thought of Elaine, dear Elaine. Ten minutes later, he was incapable of thinking of anything except the woman whose hands and tongue moved expertly around him, giving him exquisite pleasures he never knew existed.

When Steve reported for night duty two days later, there was no message from the C.I.D. He paraded as usual, was allocated a Panda patrol on the western outskirts of Pollsfield and had TC to keep an eye on him. They patrolled the town's extremities, watching for drunken drivers, troublesome youths and vandals who liked setting fire to schools or throwing bricks through shop windows. There were the inevitable trouble-spots in the town centre and several Ten Nine calls came from crews in the thick of it. He had quickly learned that a Ten Nine call over the radio meant that urgent assistance was required by the caller, and all cars raced to help him. It was a good system—help was there within two minutes of shouting Ten Nine. It was a very comforting thought.

Then he dealt with his first traffic accident. The call came from Control who asked Panda Seven to attend an R.T.A in Benedict Street.

'Papa Seven Whisky, R.T.A Benedict Street. Two vehicles, one injury Suspect O.P.L.'

Alan Templeton smiled across the darkness. 'Well, Twelve Fifteen, this one's yours. You can deal with it—the P.N.A is in the front of the car, with your Accident Booklet and Stats 19. Breathtest kits are in the rear pockets.'

Already their car was racing towards Benedict Street and TC was enjoying himself. 'Breathtest all drivers after accidents, any time of the day. This one's a suspect O.P.L. That means Over Permitted Limit—it means alcohol. Drunken driving. When you get to the scene, the two drivers will be going at each other hammer and tongs. Assess the situation, check for injuries, call an ambulance if one of them needs it, and sit the drunken one in your car. Separate the bastards, Twelve Fifteen, and take control of the situation. When they see us, they'll both come rushing over to tell their story first, and they'll each blame the other driver.'

TC's cynical approach was typical, Steve was beginning to realise. Seasoned policemen knew exactly how members of the great British public would react or behave in any given situation, and already in his young service he was beginning to appreciate that head shrinkers and school teachers were usually wrong about society. Society was rotten, he knew; people inflicted gross injuries and insults upon each other and the police were left to sort out the offal. Policemen are the dustbin men of society, picking up the pieces after nights of mayhem and stupidity.

'There we are, two cars. Two angry drivers. Two bloody fools, two damaged cars and two damaged egos. All yours, Twelve Fifteen.'

'What's first?' he felt his voice twitching with nervousness.

'Get out and tell them to be quiet. Look around the cars first, stroll around saying nothing, but looking important. It'll stop them braying at one another and they'll watch you—you're doing nothing, just getting their attention, and it gives you time to think.'

Steve smiled.

'I might need help,' he said.

'I'll be here, Twelve Fifteen, don't fret.'

The blue and white panda car, with its blue light flashing, eased to a halt and Steve noticed a little gathering of people on the footpath beside a pillar box. One car had its nose buried in the pillar box, and the other had its nose buried in the doors of the first. Two men were arguing fiercely and their personal aggravation had attracted the little crowd. It was first class free entertainment.

'Ask the crowd for their names,' TC advised. 'Tell them you need them as witnesses—they'll soon move away then.'

Nervously, Steve left the warm security of the Panda car and placed his helmet squarely on his head. He felt like a policeman now as he strode purposefully towards the crashed vehicles. As one, the drivers saw him and both hurried towards him, each gabbling accusations at the other as the audience smiled at this free show.

TC remained in the car, Steve noticed. This was Steve's job, his first traffic accident and his first test of settling a dispute.

'It was his fault, he came round that bend on the wrong bloody side ...'

'He's drunk, officer, you can smell his

breath ... going like a bat out of hell, not looking where he was going ...'

'Right,' Steve had often heard policemen begin with that word. 'Right, which car is which?'

'The mini is mine,' the first man pointed to it. It was a red mini, quite old, and its nose was crunched against the apparently immovable pillar box.

'And you, sir, are the owner of the Capri?' Steve addressed the other.

'Yes, I am. And look at it—this'll cost somebody a bloody fortune ...'

Steve ignored them for a moment and approached the little crowd of onlookers. He pulled his notebook from his pocket and smiled at them. 'Right,' he said. 'I need witnesses. You all saw what happened, did you?'

They all shook their heads. Every one of them denied seeing the incident but tomorrow every one would tell a remarkable tale at the office or factory. But his play dispersed the crowd and he smiled inwardly. This was working—TC's advice was sound.

'You, sir, the mini driver, sit in my police car, will you?'

'You're not arresting me, are you? Bloody hell, it was his fault ...'

'Just do as I say or you will get arrested. I just want to talk to you one at a time. Now do as I say. Is anybody hurt?' he asked as an after-thought.

They both shook their heads.

'Right, it's a minor accident. You, sir, the mini driver, to the car, please.'

The man obeyed without question. Steve now had control of the situation, as the man moved towards the police car. TC opened the door and invited the driver to sit down. He entered and Steve sighed with relief.

With the other driver at his side, Steve walked around the pile-up, noting that the damage was not too severe. There was a good deal of crumpled metal, one smashed windscreen and a lot of broken headlamp glass. There were no skid marks, he noted, and no damp road surface. Suddenly, all his training school theory and practice was coming home to him. Things were beginning to make sense. Measure the scene, talk to the drivers, check licences, insurance and test certificates if the cars were over three years old. Check with the P.N.C for the registered owners' names and addresses, and compare with the information provided by the drivers. There might be a stolen car or one borrowed without lawful consent.

He found himself swinging into easy routine action, talking calmly and efficiently with the Capri driver who had calmed sufficiently to talk sensibly. Steve obtained the man's name and address, issued him with an HO/RTR/1 to produce his licence, insurance and test certificate within five days and made him blow into the Alcotest 80. It showed he had drunk some alcohol, but he was well below the line.

'Thank you, sir,' he said. 'Now for the other chap.'

He repeated the procedures with the other man, who carried his driving licence and insurance. His car had not been tested, it was not yet old enough, and when he breathed into the breathalyser bag, it also showed a negative result. Both drivers were clear of alcohol, and he had all the details necessary for his accident report.

He went back to the car.

'They're all clear, TC,' he announced. 'Clean as bells. Names and addresses obtained, no injuries.'

'Easy, wasn't it? Right, what haven't you done?'

'Haven't I done?'

'Yes, what's next?' asked TC.

'They're not hurt, there's no hospital to worry about, or doctors.'

'What about the cars? Are they going to stay there all night then? You've measured the scene?'

'Yes, I've done that—oh! Breakdown truck!'

'Control will get one for you if you ask them. Are they driveable?'

Steve went back to the men.

'Is your car driveable?' he asked them both. After moving them from their position by hand, it was found the Capri could be driven after prising a wing from a tyre, but the mini was too badly damaged. Its front end was severely crumpled and oil had poured from the engine. 'I'll arrange a breakdown,' he said.

'Who's going to pay for all this?' asked the mini driver.

TC had now emerged and addressed the speaker. 'Your insurance company, sir. Tell them about this accident and they'll contact us for an abstract of this officer's report.'

'Will there be a court case then?' asked the man. 'I mean, he was coming far too fast around that corner.'

'Our prosecution department will study

this officer's report and will then decide whether or not to prosecute one or both of you. Personally, I don't think we will take any action because there are no independent witnesses. It's one man's word against another.'

Each promptly began a new tirade, but TC stemmed it by raising a hand.

'Look, fellers, it's no good arguing here. You've had an accident, we've got details. Your respective insurance companies will be supplied with details upon request. Neither of you is over the limit for drink and the Post Office will want somebody to repair that pillar box. I've arranged for a breakdown truck to come and that's all for us. This officer is P.C Crosby, he's the reporting officer. I'm just a helper.'

They waited until the breakdown truck arrived with its orange light flashing and as the Capri was driven off looking very much worse for wear, they set about hitching the battered mini to a tow bar.

Then it was meal time.

At two o'clock that morning, Steve found himself seated next to Sergeant Wilde in the canteen as they ate their sandwiches and drank their coffee. Wilde quizzed him about the traffic accident and seemed satisfied with the action he had taken. He expressed his pleasure at TC's decision to allow Twelve Fifteen to deal entirely with it. It was a simple one, an ideal ice-breaker for a young lad, and he learned a lot from it.

It was during a quiet moment that Steve decided to tell Wilde about the jeweller and his suspect thief.

THIRTEEN

Sergeant Stanley Wilde listened intently to the words of this young probationary constable and knew the Inspector would be severely critical of the lad's actions. But Wilde accepted he had acted with the best will in the world; he was not to know of the savage internal wrangling of competing police departments, of the petty internal jealousies and the continuing competition to make arrests in order to keep the annual crime figures looking decent.

'When did you tell Creaser?'

'Three nights ago, sergeant.'

'Then it's too late for us to salvage this one, Twelve Fifteen. Have you finished eating?'

'Er, yes.' Stephen drained the last of his coffee.

'Let's go downstairs and have a look at the charge book. If they've brought that woman in, it'll be logged there.'

With Stanley Wilde leading the way, they clomped downstairs to the ground floor and entered the cell area. The night gaoler, known as the bridewell keeper, was on duty and eating his sandwiches in his lonely and barren cell area. He used a little table in the passage.

'Hello, sarge, got a customer for me?'

'No, sorry, Luke. Where're the charge sheets?'

'In the front office. I'll get 'em.'

'No, sit down and finish your grub. We'll find them.'

The duty constable in the front office had the charge sheets in their huge bound book and they were spread open before him. He was checking the monthly return of arrests and bailings and entering the figures on a piece of paper headed Male and Female.

'Now, Harry, can I borrow the sheets a minute?'

'Sure, sarge,' and on a piece of paper he wrote the consecutive number of the one he was checking so he would not lose his place. 'Two hundred and five lock-ups this month. That's not bad.'

'Have we had a woman in for stealing jewellery? In the last three days? A C.I.D knock-off?'

'Yes, there was. Hang on, I'll turn it up.'

He flicked through the pages until he came across the one in question. 'Here we are, sarge. Jennifer Alice Broadhurst, 42 years old, a housewife and domestic worker of Albany Terrace. Arrested two nights ago for stealing jewellery, the property of a Miss Amelia Sinclair. Value of property, two thousand five hundred pounds. All recovered. It's in a property bag in a locker, being retained for evidence.'

'And Broadhurst?'

'Bailed out in £100 to appear at magistrates' court in three weeks.'

'Whose case?'

'C.I.D.'

'Yes, I know. Which officer?'

Harry looked at the signature on the charge sheet. 'Creaser, sarge.'

Sergeant Wilde turned to Steve. 'Say no more, eh, Twelve Fifteen? You've given them a lovely knock-off. If this woman's been nicking stuff from the Sinclair woman over a period, they'll count each piece of jewellery as a separate crime and they might get a clear-up of ten or a dozen jobs. It'll look great on their monthly return—and you get bugger all. Not even a thank you.'

Steve found himself thinking of TC's arrest a few weeks ago. These were two big arrests he could have had, two he should have had. His work and his enquiries had led to them both he was not credited anywhere. He was learning very quickly.

'Look,' Wilde took Steve by the arm and led him away after thanking Harry for his help. 'Next time you come across a job like this, tell one of us, one of your section sergeants. We'll decide what to do, and we will definitely give you the arrest. You need to know the arrest procedure anyway—you haven't chalked one up yet, have you?'

Steve shook his head. An arrest would be great right now, just the tonic he needed.

'Right, I'll tell the inspector. I'll ask him not to bollock you because you didn't know any better—you didn't, and that's genuine. Bloody Creaser should have had the courtesy to thank you and notify us, but the bastard didn't. I'll chew his balls off when I see him.'

'Sorry, sergeant.'

'Look, never apologise if you think you are right. I'm pleased at your results—you've only been with us a week or two and you've cracked two bloody good crimes, or given the lead into cracking them. That's one hell of a beginning, but there's nothing on your record to show it, is there?'

'On my record?'

'Your file, Twelve Fifteen. We keep a

file during your probationary period, for two whole years that is. You are reported on, checked, advised, interviewed about your progress and we talk to you every three months. You're due for assessment next week, I think.'

'They told us about our probationary period at Training School, sergeant. It's right we can be thrown out if we don't make the grade, isn't it?'

'It is,' Wilde sighed. 'But not many leave like that. We do our best to keep you all in, cajoling you along, helping you, training you. You'll be fine, so don't start fretting about getting the sack just because bloody Creaser nicked your crime. I'll report this one and that stolen television job you helped with, and they'll go down in your file, even though there was no arrest.'

'Thank you, sergeant.'

They had returned to the canteen and Wilde led the way in. 'While we're on the subject, how's the training going? I'm happy with the practical aspects. Your TC tells us you're doing fine. How about the paper work? Your home study papers and quarterly exams?'

'I'm enjoying them, sergeant. I like crime especially, we're onto the various forms of thefts now, and burglaries. It's much better than the initial course. The theory's far deeper and more interesting.'

'Your training sergeant is happy then?'

'He had a chat last week; yes, he's pleased.'

'Good. Well, I am pleased with you. Now, back to your beat. Where's your TC?'

Alan Templeton was downstairs filling the car's tank, and Steve joined him. 'What was all that about?'

Steve explained, telling Alan all about the lousy trick Creaser had played on him.

'They're all like that, are C.I.D,' he said. 'Look, next time you latch onto a crime, you tell me. I'll sort it out for you.'

'Yes, all right, TC.'

But he had no intentions of telling TC.

During the following three months, Police Constable Twelve Fifteen progressed in his work. His training sergeant wrote, 'P.C Crosby is a sensitive and sensible young constable. He studies hard in his spare time and contributes well during class discussions. His practical application of theoretical law is sound and based on a good deal of common sense. His examination results and home study papers show a keen grasp of the essential points of criminal law. I am pleased with his continual progress.'

On the practical side of his work, the sergeants on his section each signed a report which said, 'P.C Crosby is smart and alert. He applies himself very well to any task allocated to him, and has a pleasant manner when dealing with the public. He has a maturity beyond his years. He is never officious or overbearing, and is polite and courteous to his fellow officers, irrespective of rank. He is willing to learn and has already shown the makings of a thoughtful C.I.D officer. Enquiries initiated by P.C Crosby have led to two arrests for crime. His general progress is excellent.'

Both reports were endorsed by Inspector Sands and by the Superintendent in charge of the Sub-Division. All agreed that Twelve Fifteen was a very sound officer and an asset to Pollsfield Division. He was undoubtedly one of the best appointments in recent times.

He was sent away on a three weeks-long initial driving course which he passed, and therefore became qualified to drive panda cars and general purpose vehicles. He would need a further course of a shorter duration if he was to drive either fully equipped patrol cars or personnel carriers with loads. But the initial course did make him mobile, and it did qualify him as police driver.

No one approached him about his relationship with Barbara Pearson, but he took great care in his attempts to be discreet, and he did not allow it to progress beyond a casual affair. He went to her without passion or love, but merely to satisfy her cravings for sexual adventure and fulfilment. This was the outcome of his love for Elaine, for he worshipped the girl. This relationship developed along far stronger lines and Barbara knew of it; in fact, she approved. She once told him, during a session in her bathroom, that she was not jealous and he knew that. Once he let her know he was aware of her range of conquests, of the regular visitations by other men, she used him to gratify her own appetite, and to teach him as best she could. She enjoyed him; people went to her for sex, or she went to them, in much the same way as others sought help from bank managers, solicitors, friends or mothers. For Barbara, sex was a commodity; love was not in her vocabulary and she knew that one day, a fully initiated Twelve Fifteen would depart for the loving arms and sincere affection of a tender young girl. Barbara would then feel proud to have educated that youngster, and she would seek another. Others were plentiful—the Police Service was recruiting men as never before, thanks to the Edmund Davies pay formula and the effects of the recession. She had many years of excitement ahead.

At the end of nine months, Twelve Fifteen was fully confident of his abilities as a constable. He had arrested youths for brawling, druggies for smoking cannabis, thieves for stealing, motorists for failing breathtests, children for vandalism, yobbos for public order offences and a con man for passing a dud cheque. In addition, he had submitted offence reports for numerous Construction and Use offences relating to motor vehicles, such as bald tyres, noisy exhaust pipes, faulty horns or windscreen wipers and dangerous parts. He had booked drivers for illegal parking, for careless driving, for failing to report accidents and for driving without consideration for other users of the road. He had summonsed a Dutchman for depositing litter, a Chinese for swearing at a Catholic priest, a black youth for pee-ing in the street and a German for writing on the wall of the Labour Party offices. In short, his first few months were incredibly busy and active, and he learned more of life in those weeks than in his previous nineteen years. He had seen human nature at its worst; he had seen the inhumanity that humans could practise upon each other, the violence within marriage, the assaults on children, the rapes of women, the mugging of defenceless old ladies and gentlemen, the horror of fatal traffic accidents and the agony of accidents around the homes, the tragedy of sudden death, the appalling idleness of many and the equally appalling selfishness of others. He had attended riots and race-meetings, punch-ups and civic events. All were there in this picturesque town, mostly concealed from the eyes of the public until revealed when one of the citizens overstepped the bounds and found himself in trouble with the law.

In those fascinating weeks, Stephen Crosby's world had changed beyond all expectation. Suddenly and without ever realising it, he had become a fully professional police officer. He found himself thinking like one, acting like one and looking like one. In spite of his youth, he was in charge of his own destiny; he had learned quickly and accurately. The new Stephen Crosby was going to succeed in his chosen career.

Then at three o'clock one late summer afternoon, when the air was warm and balmy and the girls moving sensuously around the town in thin dresses and even thinner blouses, he was directed to a routine traffic accident.

'Papa Two-Five Tango. Papa Two-Five Tango. Report of R.T.A on Belford Avenue, two vehicles.'

'Ten Four,' he acknowledged and drove

to the scene, his blue light flashing and his two-tone horn blaring in familiar manner. He was alone, there was no TC now. He thrilled as the tiny car wove among the public in their dull ordinary vehicles, all wary of the message coming from the blue light and the blaring horns. He found himself at the scene well within the two-minutes response time claimed by "B" Section.

By now, he had dealt with numerous accidents; he'd never actually dealt with a fatality though, but had coped with scores of minor injury accidents. This was another. Another job, another piece of police experience.

As he had now come to expect, the drivers were standing shouting at each other while their cars were abandoned in the middle of the road with their engines running. Oil was spreading ominously beneath one of them. But this accident was different. As he approached, two white men stood their ground near a new-looking

Ford Granada, and three black men danced around their old Chrysler, hurling abuse at the white men and threatening them with violence.

Steve swallowed and felt a tremor of nervousness trickle through his body. This wasn't going to be easy. He parked his car across the centre of the road, leaving the blue light flashing to warn oncoming motorists of the blockage, and walked steadfastly towards the warring parties.

'The fuzz, man.' 'The white fuzz.' 'One of theirs, man ... there's no justice ...' 'A nigger-bashing white copper.' 'He shouldn't have survived Brixton, man.'

'Hold it,' he said, feeling very much a juvenile member of the Force once more. 'Let me talk to you all. First, anyone hurt?'

The blacks all shook their heads, and so did the white men.

'Damage?'

'My front end,' said a white man. 'Lights, radiator, front wings, bumper.

Engine too, I expect. Those bloody idiots crossed right in front of me, right across the road ...'

'I'll talk to you soon, sir,' and he now turned to address the three black men.

'Which of you guys was driving, then?'

They did not answer. They simply stood facing him, three powerful black youths in jeans and brightly coloured shirts. They had long hair in twisted strands and their thick lips were closed in silent defiance.

'They don't speak to the police,' called one of the white men. 'They told us not to bother calling the fuzz, the white fuzz, because they'd not say anything. They say you always pick on blacks because they're black.'

Steve tried again. 'Look, you guys,' he said. 'I can't help you if you won't speak. I can't make a report if you don't co-operate with me. How can you expect fair treatment if you behave like this? I need to know the driver's name, whether he's hurt or not ...'

'Piss off,' snarled one of them, showing large white teeth. 'We don't talk to no coppers.'

He looked at the others. Two more pairs of pale, reddened eyes bore down on him, full of unspoken menace and hatred. They moved all the time, shifting from one foot to the other.

He steeled himself to look into their car, opening the driver's door to check for injured people who might be inside. It was empty. He checked the damage too. The entire nearside of the car was badly damaged, the door panels and wings being buckled probably beyond repair. A wheel was lying at an awkward angle, at the front.

'Your car is damaged,' he told them. 'It's not driveable. I'm going to radio for help for you.'

'The fuzz is helping the blackman, the fuzz is being kind, the fuzz is fussing over us lads.'

The centre one quoted those words

with the metre of a poem, and Steve went to his own car. He picked up the radio.

'Twelve Fifteen,' he said. 'Are you receiving?'

'Ten Four.'

'Assistance please at R.T.A in Belford Avenue. No injuries, but I suggest supervision attend, also breakdown vehicle. Over.'

There was a long pause, and then a voice asked, 'Twelve Fifteen. Why do you need assistance? Isn't this a straightforward two-vehicle shunt?'

'No,' he said, not wishing the blacks to overhear the reason for his concern. 'It is not an ordinary accident. Supervision is needed.'

'Ten Four.'

As he waited for one of the sergeants to arrive, he spoke to the white driver.

'Are you the driver of the Granada, sir?' he needed confirmation.

'I am.'

Steve produced an accident report booklet from his tunic pocket and opened it. The three blacks came and stood close, listening to every word. The menace in their mere presence was terrifying, but the three white men faced the three blacks. The score was even.

'Name, please?' Steve began his interview. The man was honest and cool, saying his name was Lawson and he was visiting the town with his colleague when the Chrysler had suddenly turned right and driven directly across his path. It was apparently heading for the entrance of the houses. There had been no chance to stop and he had ploughed into the side of the vehicle. A passer-by had called the police while the three black men had simply stood there hurling abuse until his arrival.

'Can you identify the driver of that Chrysler?' Steve asked, without a great deal of hope.

'Yes,' said the white man. 'That one,' and he pointed to the one on the extreme left. 'He's wearing a red shirt—the others are blue, you see. There's no doubt in my mind.'

Steve carefully scrutinised the man in question, attempting to memorise his features should his identification be questioned in the future. He felt sure it would be. These characters would say he was not the driver.

Then Sergeant Henderson arrived in a small white Escort, quickly followed by a breakdown vehicle.

Steve went across to meet him and explain his predicament.

The three blacks went with him, each walking so close he could feel their breath on his neck.

'Trouble, Twelve Fifteen.'

'These men refuse to talk, sergeant. They have been involved in an accident with that car and will not provide details.'

'Hmm,' Henderson walked towards the immobilised car. 'No talking, eh? Usual tactic. Then they'll complain of police harassment, they'll ring the National Council of Civil Liberties and their underground press. They'll accuse us of racism if we ask them questions, they'll say we threatened them, and they'll say we were unfair, angry, rude, abusive ...'

'Hey, man,' said one of them. 'We's not as bad as that.'

Henderson did not reply. He asked the white men. 'Did they injure you, sir? Abuse you? Threaten you?'

'They abused us, yes. Called us every name under the sun—I've grown to expect that, officer, from black and white yobbos.'

'You callin' us yobbos, then?' one of the blacks stepped forward. Stephen put up a restraining hand, but the black youth hissed, 'You'd better not assault me, fuzz man. You had better not, or I'll complain, so I will.'

'Of course you will,' sad Steve.

'Right,' Henderson took control. 'I see it like this. These gentlemen have co-operated as the law requests,' he motioned to the white men. 'You gentlemen have not. The law specifies that in the event of an accident involving a motor vehicle on a road, the driver will furnish certain details about himself and the vehicle to any person having grounds for requiring that information, or to a police officer. If you refuse to provide that information, gentlemen,' he smiled, 'I can only assume you are disqualified drivers, or that you have stolen this car, or that you are convicts on the run, or that you are criminals going about some nefarious business.'

He paused as a police dog van cruised around the corner with two uniformed officers seated in the front. Dogs were barking in the rear.

'Criminals and suspect criminals need to be arrested to protect the public—the black and white public—so I put the question, are you criminals, gentlemen? Are you dope pedlars? Disqualified drivers? Or what?'

The dog van halted nearby and the

officers dismounted. Quickly, he opened the cage to produce two large alsatians which promptly began to snarl and bark.

'Who is the driver?' asked Sergeant Henderson, quietly.

'I am,' the one in the red shirt raised his hand.

'I want to ask you a few questions,' Sergeant Henderson put out a hand for Steve's accident report booklet.

'I'll talk in the presence of my solicitor,' said the youth.

'And where is your solicitor?' smiled Henderson.

'I'm his solicitor,' said one of the others, stepping forward.

'Am I permitted to ask this gentleman some questions about this accident?'

'You can ask his name and address, and the name and address of the owner of the car. You can ask to see his driving licence, his certificate of insurance and the test certificate. You can also ask him to make a statement, which he will refuse to do.

You have no power to ask my name or the name of the other passenger. I will not give those details, sergeant.'

Henderson smiled.

'I am so pleased you have agreed to co-operate, sir,' he said with a hint of mockery. 'Otherwise you would all be arrested on suspicion of theft of this car. Twelve Fifteen, put its number through the P.N.C as a safeguard. See if it is wanted for any reason. It could be stolen or of some other police interest.'

As Steve went off to check this detail, the black youth gave the prescribed details.

FOURTEEN

A week later, at eleven one morning while on early turn, Steve was called to the Chief Superintendent's office on the top floor. He waited outside, wondering what he had done wrong. The secretary went to announce his arrival, and within a minute he was standing to attention before the boss of Pollsfield Division. Other plain-clothed officers stood around, hands behind their backs, waiting.

He was not invited to be seated. What did they want?

'P.C Crosby,' Chief Superintendent Lloyd coughed. 'This is not a pleasant duty, not for me or for any of these gentlemen here,' and the big man reeled off the names of the men around him. Steve tried to listen to the names but the words were lost in his haze of bewilderment. No one was smiling, they were all so serious.

The Chief Superintendent continued. 'There has been a serious allegation against you, P.C Crosby. Now, on the fifteenth, did you deal with a traffic accident in Belford Avenue?'

'Yes, sir.'

'Three coloured gentlemen were involved?'

'Yes, sir, that's right.'

'Tell me what transpired, P.C Crosby?'

'You don't have to say anything,' one of the officers pointed out. 'I'm your Police Federation representative, P.C Crosby. Your friend.'

'I've nothing to hide,' he turned and spread his hands in a gesture of openness to them. 'I was called to the accident, two cars were involved. One was a Ford Granada driven by a white man, and the other an old Chrysler driven by a black man. He had two other black men as passengers.'

'Yes, go on.'

'Well, sir, I tried to obtain details from the black driver but he refused and the others came around me, in a threatening manner. They said they never talked to the police, the fuzz, they called us, the white fuzz.'

'Go on, Crosby.'

'I checked that nobody was hurt, sir, both cars.'

'Did you enter their car?'

'No, sir, just looked inside. It was empty.'

'Did you open a door?'

'Er,' he had to think about this. 'Yes, sir, on the driver's side, just to peep inside.'

'Then what?'

'They persisted in being awkward, sir, so I radioed for help. Sergeant Henderson arrived.'

'What did you do while you were waiting for him?'

'I interviewed the white driver, sir, he was fine.'

'Sergeant Henderson arrived, was he alone?'

'Yes, sir.'

'Did more police arrive?'

'Yes, sir, a dog van came a few minutes later. I think it was just passing when it stopped to see if we needed help.'

'Were the dogs barking?'

'They began to bark when the van stopped, sir.'

'Were any threats made by the police?'

'Not by the police, sir. The black men made threats to me, before the others arrived.'

'And then, when Sergeant Henderson arrived, did they co-operate?'

'One of them said he was the solicitor for the driver, and advised the driver only to give the briefest details, sir. He gave them.'

'Were threats of arrest made?'

'Not by me, sir, no.'

'By anyone else then?'

'I didn't hear them, sir.'

'Well, gentlemen?' the Superintendent turned to the man on his left. 'That's a clear account.'

The big man on his right came forward. 'P.C Crosby. I am Superintendent Precious of the Force Complaints and Discipline Department, based at Force Headquarters. I have received a complaint from a Mr Rudolph Carstairs, a coloured gentleman, and it relates to the manner in which you dealt with a road traffic accident in which he was involved. He makes two allegations—first, that you entered his car without authority and stole £400 in cash from his vehicle ...'

'He said that?' screamed Steve. 'The lying sod ... I never went in his car ...'

'And secondly, that you and other officers used harassment and bullying tactics during the interviews in connection with that accident.'

'I called for help, sir, because they were threatening me ...'

'Look, son,' the Chief Superintendent

adopted a calming voice. 'At the moment, all this is off the record. I just want to establish whether or not I need carry out an investigation into this set of allegations.'

'I just opened the car door, sir, that's all, to check for injured passengers. I didn't even lean inside ... I saw no money!'

'It's a regular event now, this sort of complaint when we come across militants of all colours and creeds. They level false complaints against the officers, just to upset our equilibrium. I'm certain this is such a complaint, P.C Crosby, but I must examine the facts. I have examined the incident log and am satisfied that no police were called in order to harass the black men—the log shows the sequence of their arrival and I have a recording of their responses over the air—and yours. It is the money that is important.'

'Sir, I've never seen that amount in my life ...'

'When trouble-makers of this kind stage a complaint, P.C Crosby, they usually do it when they've enough ammunition to make it sound genuine,' the Chief Superintendent said softly. 'You were on your own with them before Sergeant Henderson arrived?'

'The other driver was there, sir, he would see what happened.'

'You've interviewed him, Mr Precious?'

'Yes, sir, he backs P.C Crosby's story. He saw Crosby pull open the driver's door and look inside; he said Crosby never put a hand inside the car.'

'Thank you, Mr Precious,' Chief Superintendent Lloyd nodded with satisfaction. 'Well, P.C Crosby, myself and the others in this room are all satisfied that you did not steal the cash. We are also satisfied that there was no harassment. Mr Precious will now have to return to the complainant, Mr Carstairs, to ask if he wishes to make a formal complaint about your behaviour. If he does, it will be a complaint of criminal conduct, the other will be a complaint of police harassment. If Carstairs does insist, then we will have to make a full investigation. That will mean that you will be suspended from duty pending the enquiry, P.C Crosby, albeit on full pay. Now, your Police Federation representative is here—talk to him and seek his advice. None of this has gone on the record, son, it's all between you and these four walls. We must now await Carstairs' decision—I have a feeling he will retract his statements and "miraculously" find his missing cash. But the damage has been done, you have been unsettled and unnerved and that is what he seeks.'

'Should we consider booking him for wasting police time, sir? And can the Police Federation take him to civil court for defamation of character?'

'That is something the Federation will consider when all the evidence is to hand. Meanwhile, P.C Crosby, thank you for coming in.'

Someone nudged him and he turned to leave the claustrophobic room.

Outside, Sergeant Henderson was waiting. He must have been in earlier, being put through the same interrogation.

'Well, Twelve Fifteen?'

Ashen-faced and quivering with anger and fear, Steve walked along the corridor with his sergeant and told his story. Henderson listened and nodded, 'Come along, Twelve Fifteen, up to the canteen. I'll buy you a double brandy.'

The drink did him a power of good, but he felt so shaken by events, so let down by the public who demanded his help, so awfully hurt by the actions of those who would lie deliberately to ruin his new career. The world was full of evil bastards.

Even now, it was three against one. Three skilled black men telling lies about one solitary white officer, lies which would take a lot of disproving.

'Come on, son, that white driver, Lawson, cleared you. Even if it means taking this lot to court, we'll clear you.'

'But it's horrible, sarge. I'm just doing my job, nothing more. I'm out there, dealing with a road accident and for no reason at all, some militant yobbos can lose me my job. Whose side is the law on, sergeant?'

'It's on the side of the public, Twelve Fifteen. Sometimes some of us must suffer in order that the greater justice is done ...'

'If they succeed in having me suspended or dismissed for pinching a non-existent bunch of notes, I'll come back and kill the bloody lot of them. No black man will ever be safe from me again.'

'And then you'll be just like them. Do you realise some bastard policeman will have done something similar to an innocent black man? This is the result—a longstanding battle, laced with racial tension and conflict, and so it goes on and on, with innocent victims scattered along the way.'

'My career is at risk, sergeant, my career.

The only job I've had!'

'Look, everybody in this station knows what they're up to.'

'But one of them was a solicitor, or said he was.'

'He was, Twelve Fifteen. He's a solicitor, specialising in cases where blacks have been involved. But your witness is the other driver—you noticed how he held back during the interviews?'

'Yes, he did keep out of the way, didn't he?'

'He is also a solicitor, Twelve Fifteen, and he's been involved with blacks too, and with left-wing political militants who try the same rotten tricks to discredit us. He noted everything that went on, everything ...'

'Thank God ...'

'Not every young copper is so lucky, Twelve Fifteen. Now finish your drink and go back out there. Don't let this inhibit your actions, will you?'

'I'll try not to, sergeant.'

He wondered how he would deal with blacks in the future.

★ ★ ★ ★

Over dinner and in bed that night, Barbara listened to his sorrowful story. She sympathised, praised, ameliorated and fussed; she kissed and hugged, loved and exhausted him, and by midnight he felt a lot better. He realised he was not alone in such scurrilous attacks, that such an attack was part of his maturing process and that any operational police officer could suffer similar attacks and criticisms throughout his service.

She told of policemen who'd helped lonely widows, only to be accused of indecently assaulting them, of officers making arrests who were accused of thefts, assaults, indecencies and other wrongs while doing their duty, of motorists who always criticised officers who stopped them breaking the law, of women who complained about policewomen swearing or adopting lesbian attitudes.

These and thousands more complaints poured into the country's Police Complaints and Discipline Departments year in, year out. Sometimes a police officer was guilty, in which case he was rightfully drummed out of the service. The police service does not want bent coppers—a bent or evil police officer is hated just as much by the good officers as by the public he victimises, so the service makes sure villainous coppers are ejected swiftly from the ranks.

But it is the militant complaints against trustworthy officers which are the problem, and as Barbara talked to him about this, she ran her tongue and her fingers all over his fit young body, exciting him, making him happy and carefree. At midnight when he got out of bed to go back to Ma Binns, he felt much, much better. He wondered if Elaine would have had this effect upon him. She had gone over to Bridlington with her mum to visit a sick aunt. He missed her, he realised, but Barbara's skill and maturity had been a tonic tonight.

He was weekend off that Friday, Saturday and Sunday. He drove over to his mum's home on Friday and bought fish and chips for lunch. She liked fish and chips because it saved messing about with cooking on Fridays and she was pleased to see him. Dad would have his sandwiches at work with his pals, or get something at the canteen, but mum liked to come home on Fridays because the local pub made fish and chips at a very cheap price.

They talked about Dennis who was always out at night, and Anne who had found herself a new boyfriend who seemed a bit of a drip because he read The Daily Telegraph and worked in a bank. Before tea-time, Steve left, saying he would not stay the night because he didn't want to upset dad.

The real reason was that he had a date with Elaine. He drove back into Pollsfield, a trip of just over half-an-hour, and went to Ma Binns' to shave and bathe. At seven o'clock, he stopped his car on the Riverside Park to meet Elaine, got out and sat on a white-painted seat which looked across the fast-flowing water.

Behind him, a gang of noisy youths emerged from the King's Head and ran back towards the bridge, laughing and shouting in the sheer exuberance of youth. As he watched the water, he was aware of somebody walking towards him and left his seat to greet Elaine. But it was a youth. Surprised, he noticed it was young Paul Fitzgerald, the lad who put a brick through that window all those weeks ago.

'Now then, Paul,' he smiled.

'Hello, Mr Crosby,' the seventeen year old said. 'I was up there, waiting for my girl, Clare, and thought it was you what got out of that car.'

'How's things?'

Paul provided a long account of his recent life, and his pregnant sister's misery, but thanked Steve for his past help in having her lover dealt with.

'Why I came down, Mr Crosby, is this,' the lad adopted a confidential manner. 'I'm not supposed to grass on mates, but you did me a favour over that bastard Simpson.'

'I didn't, I booked you!'

'You got Charlie Simpson fixed, Mr Crosby, that's what I mean.'

'He deserved it, Paul.'

'Yeh, well, I thought I'd give you some gen. There's a bunch of gits going around doing old ladies' houses, you know?'

'Yes, I know. Breaking in and stealing their money, wrecking their furniture and so on.'

'It's three lads called Wallace, Blake and Swann. All from Pennine Estate. They go to Bellfield Youth Club—thought you'd like to know.'

There was a shout from behind them and a pretty girl in tight jeans and a yellow anorak was shouting at Paul.

'Thanks, Paul. I'll get those bastards.'

'They did my girl's granny, that's what, so you get 'em—for her this time.'

'I will, Paul. Thanks.'

And off ran Paul Fitzgerald, a nice lad who lacked the necessary family background and guidance. Steve returned to the seat. It was half-past seven and Elaine would soon be here.

He thought of the information he'd gleaned just now, and of Paul's words, 'So you get 'em,' he'd said. 'You.' Not some anonymous C.I.D man or uniformed officer. Him. Steve Crosby.

He talked to himself. 'I'll get them, Paul. Me. This time, it will be me. I'll show everybody that I can do it. I'll show the public we don't pinch black man's money, that we protect old ladies from the likes of these bastards ...'

Then Elaine was at his side.

'Day-dreaming?' she asked, sliding an arm around his neck.

FIFTEEN

It was a job *he* had to do. There must be no other involvements, no other assistance from the Force. These villains, these cruel robbers of old folks, were to be his.

In the days that followed, he took the opportunity to examine the Collator's files, the CRO list in C.I.D, the lists of suspects in the town and the list of target criminals. He asked around the station, quizzing seasoned men about the names without revealing his true interest.

It took about a week of gentle probing to assemble his basic information, and that amounted to their names and addresses. They were: Andrew Simon Wallace, aged 18 of 46 Edinburgh Road, Pollsfield, unemployed; Kent Blake, aged 18, of 97, Rutherglen Road, Pollsfield. Those two roads were close to one another. The third was Carl Edgar Swann, 19, of The White House, North Point Road, Pollsfield, an apprentice welder. He had their names and he had their addresses, so the rest would be a matter of persistence and good police work.

Both on and off duty, in those long afternoons when Elaine was at work, he haunted the streets both in uniform and in civilian clothes. He spent hours watching for them, and then learning of their actions. He hung about their streets until he was satisfied he had seen and identified each one, and that the memory of those sightings was firmly imprinted on his mind.

Wallace was a thin, gangling youth with long, unkempt hair of a straw colour; he smoked incessantly and walked over on his heels. His shoes always looked dirty and worn. Jeans and tee-shirts were his standard dress although he did possess a black bomber jacket which he wore occasionally. Blake was fatter, an ugly youth with long greasy black hair down to his shoulders and a thick, dark beard which reached right around to his ears. He was colossal in size, grossly overweight through a diet of fish and chips and his clothes seemed too tight. He wore dark clothes which somehow appeared to reduce his vast bulk, but which were never totally effective.

Carl Swann, the third member, was well built and in some respects a fairly decent youth. He was in regular work and had walked the town to get a job, not being content to exist on welfare state hand-outs. His pride wouldn't let him, but he mixed socially with these yobbos and after a drink or two, he seemed unable to resist the temptation to do exciting things, like breaking into other people's property. When sober and at work, Swann was a pleasure to know. When drunk, he was abominable.

Steve discovered they drank in the city centre at a pub known colloquially as the

Rogues' Gallery but whose licensed name was appropriately The Jolly Judge. This was the centre of activity for Pollsfield villains; detectives never entered alone, they were always in pairs and always won cat-calls of dirt, fuzz, filth, Old Bill and other loathsome names as they entered. But enter they did. Even the landlord and his wife were convicts, albeit with a range of convictions which did not bar them from holding a licence, and now and then, information did filter from here into police hands. One example was an attack on a seven-year-old girl two years earlier. She was savagely attacked and cruelly assaulted by a sex maniac and the regulars at the Rogues' Gallery found the name of the villain. They gave it to the police—men of this kind do have their standards and attacks on innocents are never condoned. It was for that reason that the three granny bashers never told the others of the true nature of their crimes. They never boasted; such was the bestial nature of their activities that they didn't talk about them.

But young Steve Crosby gleaned all this from diligently asking around and keeping his keen eyes open. He saw Paul Fitzgerald from time to time and kept the lad happy with an up-to-date report on his progress, saying he was waiting until they could be caught red-handed and sent away for a long stretch.

His dossier grew; his mates asked him what he was up to and he declined to tell them, saying it was a personal matter. None of the sergeants had any idea of his mission, and he made doubly sure the C.I.D never learned.

His observations gradually revealed a pattern to their operations. When he checked the reported crimes, he realised these rogues were robbing the old folks in the early evenings, between seven thirty and nine o'clock. More often than not, they simply arrived at a selected house and pretended they were from the gas board or the council, urgently inspecting houses for escaping gas or dripping taps or something. Many pensioners were robbed without realising it—these handy lads would dip into the money boxes, piggy banks and jugs of cash. They would lift mattresses, open cupboards and take away varying amounts from £1 to £100. On many occasions, the old folks never reported it, simply because they couldn't remember for certain how much they had hidden. If the lads were caught, they used violence. At that stage, someone learned about them. The number of unreported crimes could only be guessed.

And having robbed their aged victims— frequently on pensions day—they would adjourn to the Rogues' Gallery to spend it on themselves and their friends. A lot disappeared in the one-armed bandits and the space invader machines. They paid prostitutes and they bought drugs on pensioners' hard-won savings. They were despicable, corrupt, law-breaking, but all too common. Many of this breed prey on the helpless.

As Steve was building his dossier, his period as a probationer policeman was passing nicely along. He spent more and more time on his own, having learned rapidly from his TC, and he was very capable of submitting reports of the offences he found in town—drunks, motoring offences, petty mischiefs and so forth. All came through his book, and he was able to acquit himself well in court. The atmosphere of the proceedings did not overawe him, and indeed he relished seeing the villains put away or fined, either by the magistrates or by the Crown Court. To see a villain receive his punishment was rewarding, a form of job satisfaction.

The three-monthly reports submitted upon his progress by his sergeants and the training staff were all praiseworthy; Crosby had the makings of a very capable officer. He had learned the job very quickly and very effectively. His practical application was good, he was firm but polite with the public and with offenders, and his academic work was of a high order. Furthermore, the three black men dropped their allegations when confronted with the evidence of the white motorist, and they were charged with Wasting Police Time, with the added possibility of the Police Federation suing them for defamation of character. Things were definitely going his way.

In his private life, his obsession with Wallace, Blake and Swann had caused him to cool even more towards the sexy Barbara; she didn't mind too much because others would step into his bed-space, although she had found him very satisfying. Instead, he turned more towards Elaine, the lovely and lovable girl whose mere presence made him happy and whose patience with his shifts and odd hours of work was remarkable. He loved her dearly.

Eventually, however, his obsession did come to the notice of Sergeant Bill

Henderson. Henderson took him to one side half-way through a late turn; it was shortly after six o'clock and they were standing outside the Parish Church at St William, observing the passing show.

'Twelve Fifteen,' Henderson addressed him. 'You're up to something.'

'Up to something, sergeant?' smiled Steve, now more relaxed in the company of senior ranks.

'Yes, up to something. You're plotting, or you're scheming in some grand way. Buying a car, maybe? Plotting to get married? Your mind is on something big, I know it.'

'Just work, sergeant,' Steve remarked affably. 'I'm all right.'

'I know you're all right, you've never been so happy. Care to tell me?'

'There's nothing to tell, sergeant. I just keep going over the mass of information in my head—I've stored all sorts up there about villains in this town ...'

'Look, son, don't touch anything big on

your own, not with your length of service. If you've got some information about a crime, let us know. Crime is too big for a lad to cope with on his own, too big and too complicated.'

'I'll let you all know if it's a crime, sergeant.'

'Married, then? You're getting married and you're working out the cost? Whatever figure you think of, double it. Right?' And he laughed.

'Thanks for the tip.'

'Sincerely, Twelve Fifteen, keep in touch with us, won't you? Don't ruin everything. I've seen probationers get good tips from the public, about crime I mean, and they've kept it quiet hoping to make the big arrest. Then things have gone wrong—a messed-up arrest, injuries for the coppers, a big crook giving us the slip, crime squads up in arms, the Detective Chief Super playing merry hell about the uniform branch ...'

Henderson was so remarkably near the

truth that Steve wondered if he really knew, but this seemed only to reinforce his determination never to allow anyone else to muscle in. This was his job, for Paul had entrusted it to him. And so he kept silent. He could not trust anyone now, not even his workmates. Not the public, not anybody, not even Elaine.

It was later that same evening as he patrolled on foot, that he noticed the trio standing on a street corner near the Odeon. They were alone, and it was approaching eight o'clock on a warm evening. They were casually dressed and chattering amiably together.

Steve wished he was in civilian clothes. Right now, he was so conspicuous, so easy to see. But he must not lose them, not tonight. He had a feeling about tonight.

He waited in a shop doorway, managing to hide behind the mass of glass which formed the protruding windows. From here, he could watch them but none of their words reached his ears. They were deep in conversation and after fifteen minutes, they moved off.

As one, they vacated their position and walked down a side-street, laughing loudly. He. moved too, and strolled easily along the footpath at what the press insist upon calling the Regulation Pace. His movements were quite natural, quite normal. They were nicely ahead of him, walking nonchalantly away from the Odeon towards the park at the bottom of Convent Row. They ambled along, apparently not in any hurry, and turned into a side-street.

They did not look behind, but now they were out of sight, he must hurry. He mustn't lose them. He accelerated and strode quickly along the path until he reached Church Terrace. They were still ahead, kicking an old beer can up the road as they laughed and enjoyed themselves.

He lingered out of sight, listening to the sound of the rattling can until it echoed no longer. He peered around the corner. They had gone. He hurried after them and almost ran in his anxiety not to lose them.

At the end of the Church Terrace he found a footpath, a snicket as they called them in this locality, and they were moving along there. They were walking between high hedges which led through two fields which had been turned into pleasing parkland. As they crossed the area, they were laughing and talking and apparently unaware of his continuing interest.

Happily, the park was busy. Many people were walking along the path, providing useful screen, and he entered its narrow way, hearing the leaves brush against his tunic, as he hurried along. He was now well away from his allocated beat, but the radio tucked into his tunic would keep him in touch with Control. He could always justify absence from his beat by saying he was following suspects. He was.

And then they were gone.

At the far side of the park, the path emerged among a clump of rhododendron shrubs and the land spread across the landscape like an open field. There were long rows of terrace houses with interlinking streets and alleys, and he realised that while he had been pushing his way through that overgrown path, they had vanished. Had the bastards known? Had they been leading him along?

He stood at the far end, looking about in abject dismay. Some copper he'd turned out to be! You couldn't lose three big men like that!

He waited. For twenty long minutes he waited, but there was no sign of them. They had vanished among that jungle of houses and were lost for ever. He looked at his watch—it was eight o'clock and time to return to his beat.

You couldn't shadow villains in police uniform. They must have seen him, noticed his helmet moving along the path. Some child maybe had pointed him out to mummy. 'Look mummy, there's a policeman.' 'Hush, darling, or he'll take you away ...' But they couldn't have known he was following—even if they had seen him, they'd regard his amble as a routine patrol.

Steve regretfully turned and retraced his steps back to his beat, arriving in the same shop doorway near the Odeon. He pondered his next line of duty, and decided to hang around near the Rogues' Gallery. If they worked true to form they would come here before closing time.

As he waited, there was a flurry of activity on his radio, although the calls were not directed to him. Papa Two Nine and Papa One Five were directed to a bungalow in a street just off Hawthorn Road, but the details escaped him; judging by the sound of the ambulance sirens over the town, the emergency services had been called, and he guessed it was a traffic accident. That was the trouble with these radios—unless you were personally called, you could only hear one side of the conversation.

Half an hour later, his suspects arrived at the pub. The three panting youths dashed off a bus and ran into the welcoming portals of the Jolly Judge, and didn't give him a glance. Wallace, Blake and Swann were running true to form.

It was only when he booked off duty that he learned an old man in his eighties had been attacked this very evening and robbed of a mere £5. The poor soul had disturbed three men in his bungalow in Terry Avenue, just off Hawthorn Road, so all three had attacked him with their clenched fists. Neighbours had rallied but the attackers had vanished; no description was available.

'You callous bastards,' he hissed as he booked off duty. 'If I interviewed you now, you'd deny ever being there ... you've got to be caught in the act. I'll do it, so help me.'

Tomorrow, he was on early turn. He finished at three in the afternoon which meant he could spend the evening in civilian clothes, watching and waiting for them.

He wanted them bang to rights. He wanted them caught so that there could be no loop-hole, no escape, no lack of evidence.

They'd got five pounds tonight. It was not enough for a couple of rounds each, so they'd need more tomorrow.

And Stephen would be waiting.

SIXTEEN

Early turn next morning was very busy. There was a civic parade in the city at eleven o'clock and Steve found himself placing 'No Parking' cones along the processional route three hours before the event. Then, during the parade, he manned a traffic point in town and afterwards picked up all the cones in a van. He had time to pop into Elaine's shop to confirm their meeting tonight—seven-thirty outside the Odeon to see 'Tess' and then rushed off duty tired, dusty and in need of a shower.

By three o'clock, he had washed and shaved, bathed and rested. He decided to go down town to buy a pair of jeans and a new sweater; he was sorely in need of new clothes but never seemed to have the time to spend on shopping. Today he made the effort and he'd wear them tonight for Elaine.

By half-past four, he had found what he wanted. He'd met Brew Ten in a coffee bar, had a word with Barbara who was shopping for a dinner with a new friend tonight, bumped into an old school friend from his own village and had exchanged news about his former neighbours. Then he saw the three youths, Wallace, Blake and Swann. They were ambling through the crowds, laughing noisily and pushing smaller people off the footpath as they swaggered down the street like cowboys of old. He watched them from the safety of a crowd outside an ice-cream kiosk, three miserable bullies who preyed on the old and the feeble. He guessed they'd been drinking this afternoon, probably in a Market Place pub which was open all day.

On impulse, he decided to follow them. He was dressed in his civilian clothes—a pair of old jeans, a woolly sweater and training shoes and he carried a parcel containing his new purchases He did not look anything like a policeman and they would never recognise him out of uniform. They barged their way along the street, then ran through Marks and Spencers and out of the rear doors into the market where they bull-dozed between the crowded stalls. Three bullies, three villains. Three young men, out of control with the power of the law so much on their side. Everything except direct proof was on their side. Everything.

He kept a respectful distance as he followed them down the narrow streets, across a busy road and finally through many streets and alleys full of home-going office workers. When they emerged from the busy town, they calmed a little, and by the time they reached the suburbs they were walking normally, if a little noisily.

Eventually, they stopped at the end of a street near a telephone kiosk. He melted into the entrance of a block of flats to watch from a position of safety. They stood around for a while, idly chattering and kicking their heels. Planning? Scheming? Laughing and joking.

After twenty minutes, they moved towards a new street of bungalows. Steve moved like lightning; he came out of the shadows and flitted across to the telephone kiosk. He entered it. From there, he could look right along the street ahead, just as they had done. He picked up the handset and pretended to be talking as he watched the broad backs of the departing trio. They appeared to be growing nervous because they regularly turned about, sometimes walking backwards as if checking for followers. From the security of the kiosk, he had a clear view and began to experience a tingle of anticipation in his spine.

They suddenly turned right. Very abruptly and with no backward glances, they all turned down a short concrete path which led to a bungalow. Steve noted the path;

it was the one opposite the lamp post with a broken glass aloft. And, as before, they vanished.

Heart beating, he hurried from the kiosk, and as the heavy door swung into the closed position, he wondered if he should call the station. No, he decided, this was his show. He was going to get them, he was going to consummate the request from young Paul Fitzgerald.

His eyes never left the entrance to the bungalow and he found himself perspiring heavily. Suddenly, he shivered as the cool air of the approaching evening evaporated his quick perspiration, and walked all the faster because of it. Within seconds, he was at the end of the footpath to the bungalow and walked straight past, seeking some indication of their purpose. Maybe one of them had a relative here? It wasn't any of their homes—this was Grassington Grove, one of the small streets in Pennine Park.

As he moved past the bungalow, there

was no sign of activity. The path, he noted, led to the kitchen door which was at the side of the house. There was a garage which had closed doors. Either they had gone into the garden between the garage and the house, or they had entered through the kitchen door. The neighbours could not know because their bedroom walls backed onto this kitchen, giving privacy to people in their kitchens. Too much privacy?

He turned back. He must check. It was no good waiting. It had to be now. He retraced his steps along the pavement, turned down the garden path towards the back door and had difficulty preventing himself from breaking into a run. His heart was thumping heavily, the excitement rising and he thought of turning back to ring the station. Help may be needed, there were three of them.

He looked around. There was no one. The street was deserted, they had chosen well. A deserted street with a quiet bungalow whose kitchen door faced a blank wall. Was it an old person's home? There were no children running about among the houses, no teenagers talking on street corners or cleaning motor bikes, no men hosing lawns or women hanging out clothes. It was a quiet street, a street occupied by pensioners.

He knocked on the kitchen door, having first peered through the window. The kitchen was empty, save for a completed meal on the table. A meal for one. The inner door was standing wide and then he wondered about the front door. If he went in the back, they'd bolt through the front. Or they'd hide. He didn't know what they'd do ...

Should he knock? Suppose they were legitimate callers? Suppose he entered and found himself caught as a trespasser? He should have contacted the office. God, it had all sounded so simple but it wasn't. Henderson had been right. Now he knew why they were so careful in their training of young policemen. It was so risky allowing them out alone. They put themselves at risk and they risked the reputation of the Force. But he couldn't abdicate now.

He was here and he must act.

He opened the door gently. It moved easily, making no sound. Inside, there were muffled voices beyond the kitchen. He closed the door silently and turned the key locking it, then padded across the tiled floor. Voices came from somewhere inside, muffled and low, then a shout. A terrifying shout.

'Come on grandad, tell us where the bloody money is! We know you've got some hidden away. If you don't tell us, we'll knock the living daylights out of you, we'll wreck this place, smash your furniture ...'

The bedroom. They'd taken the poor old sod into the bedroom. Think, Twelve Fifteen, for God's sake think! Lock 'em in? Don't let 'em escape. Save the old man. Arrest them. All three?

Telephone? There was no telephone; he knew that instinctively because there was no line coming to the house. Observation. They'd taught him something about observation at training school.

A cry of alarm. A thumping sound. More cries. He moved. He could not wait, he must not dally.

He picked a bottle of lemonade from a shelf and advanced. Through the lounge, into the bedroom. The door was open. The front door was nearby. He padded across and locked it. Now they were his prisoners. He saw the alarm button on the wall of the interior passage. An old folks' button, linked to a local warden's house for them to press if they wanted help. He pressed it hard. He kept his finger firmly on it for at least ten seconds and then he heard the old man cry with pain and fear. He burst into the bedroom.

'Police,' he shouted. 'Police, you're all under arrest.'

He filled the doorway, holding the bottle

by its neck as they broke their attack. The old man lay on the floor, panting and making a horrible noise as the three bullies stood looking at the teenager in jeans with the bottle in his hand.

'Cop? You? Don't be bloody stupid ... this is your grandad, isn't it, son? Look, out of the way or we'll kill you. All we want is money.'

Steve smashed the bottle on the door jamb to provide him a vicious jagged glass weapon. He remained in the doorway, defiant.

'I am P.C Twelve Fifteen Crosby,' he spoke slowly and with surprising calm. 'You are all under arrest. The van is on its way. You will remain here, all of you. I'm arresting you for burglary and assault on this gentleman.'

'It is the bloody fuzz!' cried Swann.

'We have been following you for a while,' he said, in a quiet voice. 'Andrew Simon Wallace, Kent Blake and Carl Edgar Swann. We know all about you, and we've been waiting for this chance to put you away. Now, lift him up, put him on the bed.'

'Sod off, you bloody idiot!' snarled Wallace. 'You're alone, you think you can hold us ...'

'The first one to get within reach of this bottle gets his jugular vein slashed. Accidentally, of course,' he added. 'Pick him up.'

'Do as he says, Andy,' called Swann quietly. 'The old man's in a bad way.'

Steve stood his ground, wanting to go to the aid of the victim but knowing it would permit their freedom. He must remain here, with the bottle.

Blake and Swann lifted the old man onto his bed, surprisingly gently having regard to their past actions. They laid him with his head on his pillow, and Steve shouted at him, 'Police. I'm a police officer, sir, and these men are under arrest. Our men are on the way. We'll soon have you looked at by a doctor.'

The reply was a long sigh and a slight moan of pain.

'Look, young fuzz man, let us go. We've taken nothing, he's going to be all right,' and Wallace edged nearer to Steve.

'Remember that soft throat of yours, Wallace,' and Steve waved the dangerous bottle. 'Get back.'

'But we've learned our lesson,' said Blake. 'You've got us, mate, bang to rights.'

'No, I haven't. You'll be bang to rights when the court sends you all down, for this and those other jobs. All recorded, lots of them,' and then Steve saw a man walking past the bedroom window, peering in.

'Are you the warden?' he shouted.

'Yes,' came the reply.

'Get the police quick. These are three burglars, they're under arrest. Tell them to send a car, I'm P.C Crosby.'

The man vanished like lightning.

'You cunning little bastard,' snarled Wallace. 'They aren't coming at all ...'

'They are now,' smiled Steve, waving the bottle and never allowing his eyes to leave them. 'They are now.'

'Three of us against one skinny kid cop,' Wallace began his advance. 'If we can't get him before his pals come, I'm a Dutchman ...'

Steve felt nervous. God, they *were* going to come ...

He said nothing, but kept his eyes on each of them, regarding Wallace as the most dangerous. He didn't speak any more but simply stood in the bedroom doorway with the jagged bottle at the ready, daring them to come.

'Look, son,' said Wallace, only months older than Steve. 'We're not going in. Make no mistake about it. When your mates come, we'll be ready for them, won't we lads?'

'Definitely,' said Swann, moving towards the outer wall and creeping towards the window.

'It's locked,' Steve said. It was. All the

316

ground floor windows had locks on them.

'Bastards ... bloody coppers ... minding everybody's business.'

Then the welcome sound of sirens as two police cars raced to the scene. Steve heard them pull up outside, he heard the anxious shouts of the warden and running feet. A sergeant from 'C' Section appeared at the bedroom window.

'P.C Twelve Fifteen, "B" Section, sergeant,' he shouted. 'These men broke in and burgled this house, they've attacked this man and he needs help.'

'How many?'

'These three.'

'The doors are locked, Twelve Fifteen. Have you the keys?'

'Yes, in my pocket. Are the doors all covered, sergeant?'

'Sure, Twelve Fifteen. We've got 'em. Let us in.'

Steve turned away, pleased at the success of his mission, and he realised his error. With a tremendous crash of feet,

Wallace took advantage of his momentary distraction and ran at him. He launched himself at the young policeman and sent him crashing to the floor, as the jagged bottle rolled away. And Wallace seized it.

In a trice, the lad had a painful armlock on Steve.

'Now it's my turn, bastard,' he snarled. 'Now we are definitely leaving—free. And you're with us. Now move, sonny. Open that bloody door.'

SEVENTEEN

'Open the door!' bellowed Wallace again. 'Carl, get the bloody keys off him.'

In the bedroom, the old man groaned but there was no one to tend him; with the vicious armlock threatening to rip apart his shoulder muscles and with the tip of the jagged bottle pricking his neck, Steve passed the back door key to Swann. Deftly, Swann opened the door. There was a policeman outside and he looked surprised and horrified at the spectacle before him.

'Get ...' began Steve.

'Shut it!' Wallace pricked him ominously. 'Now, walk. Get us a car, all of us ...'

'You'll never get away ...'

'We will, if we have you,' and as a reminder he prodded his prisoner, his two silent colleagues following nervously. 'Car, I said, mate. A car, get a car.'

The unhappy constable on the door stood aside as Steve emerged from the shelter of the house. Police cars were waiting in the street, a panda car and a supervision car, one marked with police insignia and the other plain white. Steve's neck hurt as the sharp jagged tips of glass threatened to sever his arteries.

The sergeant came nervously towards them, and Wallace pressed the glass into Steve's neck, putting the onus on his prisoner.

'Keep back, sergeant, please,' Steve cried. 'He's got a broken bottle in my neck ... he wants a car.'

'Who are you, son?' the sergeant asked, apparently ignoring Wallace and his threat.

'Crosby, Twelve Fifteen. "B" Section, I ...'

'Just get the bloody car, son,' snarled Wallace. 'And quickly.'

'They want a car to get away, sergeant,'

Steve was perspiring and had to twist his head awkwardly to speak. 'And there's an old man in there who needs help.'

The sergeant continued to be unmoved by Wallace's dangerous stance.

'No car,' he said. 'There is no car for you.'

'Then I push this bloody bottle right into his neck,' snarled Wallace, removing it and waving it in the air to show just how terrible a weapon it had become. 'One quick jab and he's a gonner, jugular vein cut right in two.'

'You'll be caught and shot before you've gone two miles,' the sergeant spoke quietly. 'The moment you drive away from here, we will get on our radios and armed police will follow. Owing to your dangerous nature, they will have instructions to shoot to kill.'

'Then this baby fuzz dies,' and the bottle returned to Steve's neck, cold and vicious just behind his ear. 'Car, sergeant, now.'

The sergeant came forward and handed

the car keys to Steve. 'It's all right, Twelve Fifteen, we'll get him.'

'Which car?' Steve's voice was cracking.

'The panda.'

'Move!' and the bottle pressed into his neck, pricking it ever so slightly. Steve inched towards the waiting panda car, a Ford Fiesta, as Wallace ordered, 'Carl, you drive.'

As the others ran to the car, Wallace told Steve to hand over the keys. The sergeant and other officers watched at a distance as two constables entered the bungalow to tend to the victim, and Steve was bundled roughly into the rear seat. Wallace followed with the bottle always ready as Swann and Blake sat in the front.

'Where to?' Swann asked.

'Anywhere, just get the hell out of here,' snapped Wallace. 'Now, if your colleagues follow, son, you're dead. Did you hear that, sergeant,' and he shouted out of the window, 'If you follow me, this kid fuzz dies. Get it?'

Swann started the engine and the car moved off with Steve crushed into the corner as the bottle was held against his neck. This time, the smooth cool sides touched him as the vicious points were held aside. The car cruised through the town, and the sergeant did not follow it.

'Where the hell are we going?' demanded Swann.

'Anywhere—bus station, railway station, taxi ranks, any bloody where.'

'They'll see this car and follow. Andy, we've had it, honest. There's no way we'll get out of this ...'

'Great North Road then. Go for the A1. We can reach open country there. Drive like hell, these cop cars can go like hell. Open it up, Carl. A1 it is. We'll go south, away from here.'

Carl accelerated and the car responded. Soon, the town was left behind and the well-tuned car sped through open countryside. There were no police cars behind. They were alone.

As they drove, Blake was fiddling with the radio and quickly discovered how it operated. He switched it on and smiled. 'We can listen to them chasing us,' he beamed with pride.

'They won't chase us, will they, son?' Wallace insisted on calling Steve 'son', even though they were about the same age.

'No, not now,' Steve agreed. 'You've got away.'

'And what do we do with you, son?' he asked, pressing the cold bottle tight into Steve's throat.

'Ditch me,' he said. 'You've made it, you're free. Dump the car somewhere on the A1, nick yourselves another and that's it—you don't need me any more.'

'Balls!' snarled Wallace. 'You are our ticket to freedom, fuzz boy. We do need you. If they stop up or follow us, you're going to get us away, aren't you?'

'I haven't much choice, have I?'

'No choice at all, fuzz boy!'

'Are you really a copper?' asked Carl Swann. 'You look too bloody young. And those at the house didn't know you.'

'They're on a different section. We work in sections and we don't often see the others at the nick. I'm new anyway.'

'But you are a copper? Not a special or a cadet?'

'No, a full time professional copper.'

'Off duty?' asked Kent.

'Yes, off duty.'

'Then why follow us? Why come into the old geezer's like you did ...?'

'To arrest you. I don't like creeps who attack old folks, that's why, and I decided to get you.'

'It didn't work, did it, fuzz boy?' smiled Wallace. 'We're too clever.'

'It was worth a try,' Steve recognised the wisdom of apparently agreeing with this dangerous crew.

Swann drove very well. He was a natural driver and even in the police car, the four youths attracted little attention from passing motorists. Swann guided them through the busy traffic, but said, 'Hey, copper, there's nothing on this radio about us. There's all the other crap but not us.'

Steve knew the answer. The police would have anticipated them listening in and would be observing radio silence about the kidnap on this channel. They would be operating on Channel 7, and fully in touch with one another.

'They'll be having a conference,' he said hopefully. 'They'll be deciding what to do.'

'What will they do?'

'They might wait until you abandon this car,' he said. 'And circulate your descriptions, once they know I'm safe.'

'But why no reports on this radio, fuzz boy?'

'I don't know, maybe we're getting out of range. This is a panda car radio, only used in small areas. It's not a county-wide set, and the stuff you're receiving is county stuff, not local to Pollsfield.'

They lapsed into a long silence and Steve wondered if they realised the futility of their actions. There was nowhere they could go, no place where they could safely hide. Certainly, they could never return to Pollsfeld without being arrested. They had no money, no clothing, nothing.

They drove for almost an hour and never saw a police vehicle. The 'B' class road which carried them towards the A1 had grown quiet with little traffic and it seemed as if the whole world was unaware of the little drama being played out in the tiny car. For Steve himself, it seemed unreal. It was like a plot from a television drama or just a bad dream. But it was neither. It was terribly real. He was definitely in the back seat of a police car with a broken bottle nudging his throat and surrounded by thugs who seemed hell-bent on destroying themselves, and him with them.

And then suddenly there was more drama. Quite unexpectedly it was all action. A road block barred their way.

Two shining white police cars with officers at the wheel were parked right across the carriageway; one had moved into position as their little vehicle approached, having let the previous traffic through, and at the side of each one stood a tall police officer armed with a powerful rifle.

And as they approached, two more cars emerged from lanes at each side of the road, effectively closing the carriageway behind them and sealing off all other traffic.

'The bastards ... the cunning evil bastards ...' Wallace turned the savage bottle and placed its cutting edges tight against Steve's neck. He jerked away from its threat but the bottle moved with him. 'They knew ... they knew where to stop us ...'

'You'd better give yourselves up,' Steve said quietly. 'If not, they'll shoot.'

Swann braked and began to ease the car to a halt at which Wallace screamed, 'Crash through them, crash through them.

Knock those bloody jam-sandwiches aside ...'

'Don't be an idiot, Andy.' Swann halted the Fiesta. 'It's all over.' He pulled up, climbed out and placed his hands on his head. Blake followed suit, never faltering. Two officers came and took them away.

'I'm not going in, fuzz boy, not me. They'll have to carry me home dead. I'm not surrendering.'

'They'll kill you, Andy,' Steve said. 'Look, you're only my age—you've a lot of life left. Hell man, don't throw it away. This job'll get you two or three years at the most, then you'll be free to live. For God's sake don't give up, don't make them kill you. They will, that chap on the left with the rifle is a right bastard. Remember that villain who held the girl hostage in that flat? He shot him. Clean through the heart.'

'I don't want to be shut away, for God's sake. Not me, not at nineteen ...'

'Then go quietly.'

Wallace sighed heavily. 'I'm in a right mess, aren't I? Get out, fuzz boy. Come on, move!' and he jabbed Steve with the glass.

Steve climbed from the car and the bottle followed just touching his bare cheek as Wallace clambered from the cramped position. 'Stand still, fuzz boy.'

With the bottle pricking his cheek, Steve waited. Wallace stood at his side, surveying the police cordon which surrounded them. His pals were under arrest and sitting in separate cars. A small knot of motorists had gathered to watch the drama. He stood there, the centre of attention with a broken bottle in his hands and guns all around.

Suddenly, Wallace thrust the bottle into Steve's cheek. He felt the gash, the sharp cut as the pointed barbs bit into his soft flesh. He fell to the ground, bleeding profusely from severe cuts on the left of his face, and saw Wallace galloping for freedom. He cried out with shock and pain, putting his hand to his face and feeling the hot, sticky blood. There was a loud barking, someone shouting, a shot fired into the air and two police dogs leapt into action as men rushed to Steve's aid.

Someone found a pressure point on his neck; policemen were rushing everywhere, radios were calling for ambulances and the dogs never stopped barking.

★ ★ ★ ★

When the Chief Constable came to visit him in hospital, Elaine was proudly at his side. His face was a mass of dressings.

'Well?' asked the Chief. 'How are things today?'

'Fine, thank you, sir.'

'Crosby, you did a bloody stupid thing and you ought to be disciplined for being so bloody stupid. You put lives at risk, you went your own way regardless, you broke every rule about being a probationary police officer and you finish up in hospital with a cheek cut to ribbons. But it was a bloody good show, lad. Excellent. We need men like you. I liked the way you acted, it does good to break the rules now and again ...'

The Chief Constable went on at some length about rules and regulations, about standards of behaviour and risks that had to be taken, and he went out thanking the teenage policeman yet again.

Elaine kissed him on his good cheek. 'I waited ages for our date,' she said. 'I thought you'd stood me up, and then Carpet Cleaner told me about you,' and she kissed him again. 'Is this what it's going to be like, being a policeman?'

'Not all the time.' He tried to smile but the pain was awful. His skin was tight with stitches.

'There's somebody outside wants to see you,' she said. 'But they let me in because I was here first.'

'Who's out there?' he asked, his cheek hurting every time he talked.

The door opened and in walked his father, with mum close behind.

'Hello, son,' said his father, coming to the bedside.

This Large Print Book for the Partially sighted, who cannot read normal print, is published under the auspices of

THE ULVERSCROFT FOUNDATION

THE ULVERSCROFT FOUNDATION

. . . we hope that you have enjoyed this Large Print Book. Please think for a moment about those people who have worse eyesight problems than you . . . and are unable to even read or enjoy Large Print, without great difficulty.

You can help them by sending a donation, large or small to:

The Ulverscroft Foundation, 1, The Green, Bradgate Road, Anstey, Leicestershire, LE7 7FU, England.

or request a copy of our brochure for more details.

The Foundation will use all your help to assist those people who are handicapped by various sight problems and need special attention.

Thank you very much for your help.